PENGUIN HANDBOOKS
THE PHONE BOOK

LARRY KAHANER is a correspondent for McGraw-Hill World News in Washington, D.C., where he covers the telecommunications industry for *Business Week* magazine. He also has written for *The Village Voice, High Technology, Science Digest, Washington Journalism Review,* and *Popular Science.* As a reporter for The Columbus (Ga.) *Ledger,* he received several awards for his investigative reports on southern textile mills. This is his third book.

ALAN GREEN, who previously covered telecommunications for *Broadcasting* magazine, is editorial director of The City Desk, a Washington, D.C.-based bureau for city and regional magazines. His work has appeared in dozens of magazines and newspapers, including *The New Republic* and *The Washington Post.* In addition, he is Washington editor of *Videography* magazine.

The PHONE BOOK

THE MOST COMPLETE GUIDE TO THE CHANGING WORLD OF TELEPHONES

BY LARRY KAHANER & ALAN GREEN

A Tilden Press Book

PENGUIN BOOKS

Penguin Books Ltd, Harmondsworth,
Middlesex, England
Penguin Books, 40 West 23rd Street,
New York, New York 10010, U.S.A.
Penguin Books Australia Ltd, Ringwood,
Victoria, Australia
Penguin Books Canada Limited, 2801 John Street,
Markham, Ontario, Canada L3R 1B4
Penguin Books (N.Z.) Ltd, 182–190 Wairau Road,
Auckland 10, New Zealand

First published 1983

Printed in the United States of America by
R. R. Donnelley & Sons, Crawfordsville, Indiana

Illustrations by Ron Carnahan

To Tom Watson,
who came when Alexander Bell wanted him

CONTENTS

The White Pages

The Yellow Pages

A complete listing of companies, agencies, and associations related to telephone products and services.

Acknowledgments

The authors wish to thank several people for their help. Some offered information when we wanted it; others offered an ear when we needed it: Ev Clark, Bernie Goodrich, Bill Hogan, Patricia Jones, Diane Kiesel, Don McLaughlin, Doug Starr, and Paul Travis.

We also want to express special appreciation to Joel Makower of Tilden Press, Gerald Howard of Penguin Books, and literary agent Raphael Sagalyn, each of whom brought his own unique brand of enthusiasm and skill to this project.

—L.K. and A.G.
Washington, D.C.
February 1983

How To Use This Book

For many of us, the new world of telephones has become confusing and bewildering. This book will help make sense of it all, as telephones enter a new era of high-tech, high-priced equipment, and a dazzling list of options and services that go with it.

Even with all the facts, though, utter confusion is still possible. To help you set things straight, we've divided this book into two parts: The White Pages will give you information to help make intelligent decisions, detailing, among other things, the types of telephone equipment available, how to shop for long distance services, how to install your own equipment, and how to avoid paying more than you should. The Yellow Pages will help you track down all the gadgets and services that pique your interest.

Nearly everything mentioned in The White Pages can be found in The Yellow Pages, and we've cross-referenced The Yellow Pages so you won't have to go fishing around in the dark. We didn't list every pertinent company or supplier; rather we singled out some of the major firms in each category.

If you don't find exactly what you're looking for, don't assume it doesn't exist. The lid on this market has recently been ripped off, and new products and services are arriving daily. If one company doesn't have it, call another.

The

WHITE PAGES

INTRODUCTION

Forget everything you've ever known about telephones.

That ever-present purveyor of long distance and long windedness, found in more than 98 percent of American homes, is undergoing a vast change. Already, a growing number of Americans are required to buy, rather than rent, their new phones. And soon after the government-ordered break-up of AT&T is completed, you may receive two separate phone bills—one for local phone calls, the other for long distance calls. Moreover, you will be asked to choose which of several long distance phone companies you want to do business with.

The simple taken-for-granted telephone is turning into the high-tech, high-interest—and, in many cases, high-priced—consumer item of the 1980s. Increasingly, you'll be choosing from hundreds of companies offering telephones, accessories, and a mind-boggling array of services.

Telephones are your entry into the information age. You can choose phones that travel with you around the house or around the world, and phones that let you travel through computer banks containing the world's knowledge.

The potential ramifications of the telephone explosion are staggering:

- At last count, little more than 5 percent of the nation's 180 million phones were customer owned; by 1986 that figure will top 95 percent.
- By 1985, the market for telephones and related products and

services will grow to $95 billion—an increase of nearly 50 percent since 1982.

- Five years ago, only two long distance companies competed with AT&T. Now, more than 200 companies offer such services.
- By the end of 1982, there were only 150,000 mobile phones in the U.S. A new, sophisticated mobile phone service will boost the number of mobile phone users to 3 million within the next five years.
- Pocket pagers (known also as "beepers"), previously restricted only to local service, are now available for both national and international service. And, they don't just beep; the new generation of pagers provide printouts or flash written messages on their tiny screens.
- Newly available telephones allow you to store hundreds of phone numbers that you dial at a punch of a button. Other phones store, then forward your voice messages to others even if you're out of town. Still other phones automatically screen your incoming calls, letting through only those that you desire.
- Some banks and stores already let you transact business by phone, reaching their computers from your own home. Within the next ten years, we will buy, sell, and trade more than a billion dollars' worth of goods and services annually over the phones.

The first era of telephone technology is nearly at an end, and the future will in no way resemble the past. For the first time, there will be stiff competition, and you won't have one phone company—namely, Ma Bell—to complain to (or complain about) anymore.

In short, it's up to you, the consumer, to get your money's worth.

It's your dime.

GOOD-BYE, MA BELL

It's simple: You dial the phone number, someone answers, and you talk.

Right? Well, yes. But it's really not so simple once you take a closer look.

Our telephone system is the most extensive communications network in the world. In the United States alone, it consists of 970 million miles of wire strung on 20 million poles, 500,000 miles of underground cable, 250,000 miles of microwave relay stations, 180 million phones, 30,000 local switching offices, and dozens of satellites. It employs more than one million people and takes around $40,000,000,000 each year to keep running. It connects more than 600 million conversations every day. Ninety-eight percent of American homes have at least one phone. It's nothing short of a miracle.

The miracle starts at your home or business where a telephone is wired to a main junction box—usually in the basement or on the outside of the building—before heading into the street. There, it meets up with other lines just like it, and they all travel together under the ground or suspended by poles to the telephone central office. (Actually, the wire from your phone doesn't travel directly to the central office. Your neighborhood is covered by a matrix of wires into which your phone line connects. But for all practical purposes, it's as if your line goes directly to the central office.)

Each central office handles phone numbers that begin with the same three digits. Those digits are called the "exchange." In the good old days, exchanges carried colorful names like Cloverdale, Esplanade, Murray Hill, and Twining, but now the number-equivalents of the first two letters plus another number take their place.

At the central office, your phone's wires and those of others in your exchange are hooked up to switches. When you pick up your telephone handset and the little receiver buttons pop up, a switch opens at the central office and searches for a dial tone. That's the slight click you hear in the receiver before you hear a dial tone. Unless the exchange is extremely crowded with calls, finding a dial tone takes less than a second. (We're lucky: In some countries, it takes a minute or more.)

When you dial a number, the switch opens and closes very quickly for each number dialed. In fact, if you're fast enough, try this experiment: Dial a friend's phone number by pressing down the receiver buttons very quickly—five times for the number five, a short pause, then two times for the number two, pause, and so on. It really works. A Touch-Tone phone accomplishes the same fast on-off action by using a system of tones that are converted at the central office to on-off pulses.

If you're dialing a number within your exchange (the same first three digits) the switches connect you to the proper set of wires elsewhere in that central office for the phone number you're calling. However, if you're calling a different exchange, the switches route your call outside to the appropriate central office. At one time, the switches were mechanical. That made them very slow. Now, almost all switches are electronic and the latest ones can handle 100,000 calls a second.

Many businesses install phone systems in their offices called PBXs, or "private branch exchanges." They act like small, private central offices that handle only the phones in the office. That's why in a PBX-equipped office you don't need to dial all seven digits of a nearby desk, just the last four, or sometimes the last two. And when you're calling outside the office, you must first dial a designated digit, usually a "9," to get a dial tone outside your own little "central office."

If you're calling long distance, the central office switch recognizes the first three digits as an area code number (because the second number of an area code is always a "1" or a "0") and not an exchange number, and it automatically connects your phone to a long distance switching office. The long distance office may be close or it may be several miles away. From there,

How A Long Distance Call Works

When you call long distance from City A, the local central switching office automatically sends your call to a long distance office. From there, the call is routed via cable, satellite, or microwave radio to a long distance switching office in City B. The call then goes back into a local office in City B, and electronic switches help it find the wires connected to the phone you're calling.

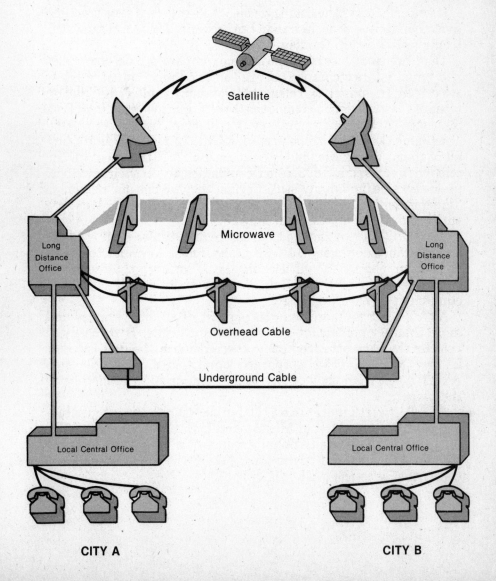

the call is routed via cable, satellite, or microwave radio to another long distance switching office near the phone you're calling. Once there, your call goes back into another central office, and electronic switches help it find the wires connected to the particular phone you're calling.

The same procedure happens if you're calling overseas. The only difference is that the long distance part covers more territory. Usually, satellites are used, but sometimes, depending upon how much telephone traffic there is, your call could go by underwater cable.

If you call across the country, this whole process takes less than five seconds; overseas, less than ten seconds. The fast-acting electronic switches are the key.

There are two types of phone service companies: local companies and long distance companies. As the telephone industry grew, American Telephone & Telegraph Company built or bought up most of the local phone companies (New York Bell, Mountain Bell, Southern Bell, Pacific Bell, etc.) and they became the Bell Telephone Companies, one part of AT&T. But AT&T didn't buy all of them. When Alexander Graham Bell's 1876 patent on the telephone expired in 1893, other companies began their own local phone service, and many still survive; they've become known as "independents." About 1,500 independents still exist. Most are small and many are in rural areas.

But as AT&T bought the local companies, it also built the only long distance company—AT&T Long Lines. And just to round out this monopoly, it built the biggest laboratory that develops telephone equipment, Bell Labs, and the major supplier of phone equipment, Western Electric.

AT&T controls more than 80 percent of all local phones and more than 94 percent of all long distance calls. It owns more vehicles than any other company. Its trademark, the Bell, is better known than any other corporate logo. And more people own AT&T stock than that of any other company in the history of the planet.

AT&T is worth more than $150 billion—that's three times bigger than Exxon, General Motors and U.S. Steel *combined*. It's bigger than the gross national product of all but a dozen countries. AT&T's annual profit tops $6 billion.

But that was the past.

Good-bye, Ma Bell

The world's largest and richest monopoly, AT&T—the company founded by Alexander Graham Bell that has controlled the telephone industry almost since Day One—is finally being dissolved. For you, the consumer, it's great: you now have a choice. No longer will someone tell you what you must buy and from whom you will buy it. For the first time in American history, we have growing competition in the telephone industry.

The United States has the best phone service in the world. There's little doubt about that, but we paid a very high price for it. One company has virtually run the industry, decided what services to offer, what products to manufacture, what technical standards the industry will use, and, most important, what prices to

charge. It did this, in large part, because it not only controlled 22 of the largest local telephone companies, the Bell Telephone Companies, but also the country's long distance network.

In the U.S., phone companies have been treated much like gas or electric utility companies. In exchange for an exclusive franchise to serve the public, a utility company must provide a certain level of service under government supervision. At the same time, the company receives a guaranteed income. That's how it's been with AT&T.

Unfortunately, this arrangement doesn't usually work to consumers' advantage. Utilities are not always responsive to consumer complaints because they are the only game in town, when it comes to their product or service, and regulatory agencies don't always have the ability—and sometimes the desire—to keep track of companies' actions. That's especially true for a company with the enormous size, wealth, and power of AT&T.

This great influence and lack of government controls has meant that AT&T didn't have to worry about any new competition. When other companies wanted to start long distance service, AT&T simply didn't let them connect into local phone systems. Without that local connection, even E.T. couldn't phone home. So these long distance companies took AT&T to court and finally won the right to connect to the local Bell Telephone Companies. MCI, the first such company, won its landmark case in 1969; more about them later on.

While long distance companies were fighting for the right to connect into AT&T's local network, the independent phone companies fought for the right to connect their phones to AT&T's long distance network, so their local customers could call cross country. AT&T didn't want to do that either, but the independents banded together and finally won the right to connect to AT&T Long Lines.

AT&T wasn't very nice to certain other folks, either. It has been accused of stifling its telephone equipment competition by mandating that its local phone companies buy only from Western Electric, the phone manufacturer owned by AT&T. Other manufacturers, many of which make excellent phone equipment, could not sell their wares to Bell companies because of this discrimination. In fact, AT&T went so far as to prohibit any non-Western Electric product to connect to any Bell System telephone, claiming that it would damage the "integrity of the network," as they liked to call it. Ma Bell even resisted something as simple as a product called "Hush-A-Phone" from being placed by customers on telephone handsets. The "Hush-A-Phone" was a simple rubber cushion placed over the mouthpiece to prevent people nearby from overhearing your conversation. In 1956, AT&T insisted, all the way to the U.S Court of Appeals in Washington, D.C., that this little foam cushion could threaten the nation's phone network. The court didn't see it quite that way; AT&T lost the case.

But it wasn't until 1968 that consumers won the right to connect non-Western Electric devices to their home or business telephone systems. It took a man named Thomas Carter more than a half-dozen years to win consumers that right. The breakthrough was named the "Carterfone Decision" after Carter's device, which connected two-way radios to the phone system via

Who's Who In Telephones

It's hard to tell the players without a scorecard, particularly when a number of new names and faces have arrived on the telephone industry scene. To set the record straight, here's a summary of who's who in the new telephone environment:

- American Telephone & Telegraph is still known as AT&T, although as of January 1, 1984, the Bell System's 22 operating companies are seven independent regional companies providing local phone service only.

- The operating companies have no common corporate name, but each may include the word "Bell" in its official title and familiar Bell logo.

- As of January 1, 1984, AT&T can no longer provide local telephone service, but it can offer a host of other products and services. It will retain its long distance facilities (AT&T Long Lines), its research and development facilities (Bell Labs), and its manufacturing division (Western Electric).

- AT&T is now able to market telecommunications products under a new unregulated subsidiary, American Bell Inc.—known also as "Baby Bell." American Bell is divided into two divisions, each with separate responsibilities: the consumer products division sells equipment to consumers at retail phone stores around the country; Advanced Information Systems (AIS) markets equipment to the business community.

- Another new AT&T subsidiary, Advanced Mobile Phone Service (AMPS), offers cellular radio services.

a base station. That led to the sale of non-Bell answering machines that became popular in the early 1970s. Slowly, AT&T lost its stranglehold on the telephone industry.

And that brings us to today.

Despite these time-consuming but major victories against AT&T, true competition could never be accomplished in a piecemeal way, the government decided. After trying to break AT&T's grip on the nation's phone service for decades, including several lawsuits in the 1930s and 1940s that ended in out-of-court settlements, the Justice Department took AT&T to court in 1974 for violation of antitrust laws. This time it meant business.

The government's primary goal was to sever once and forever the all-too-cozy tie between local Bell companies (the companies that wire the phone into your home) from AT&T's long distance service (the company that wires the local telephone companies to each other). The government figured that by separating the local phone companies from AT&T, Western Electric, and Bell Labs, it would halt, among other things, the unfair buying practices that prevented the local Bell companies from purchasing equipment—often, lower priced equipment—from companies other than Western Electric. These savings could be passed along to telephone customers, said the Justice Department.

Clearly, the situation was unfair. It would be like one Detroit automaker building all the cars and owning all the gas stations. And, at the same time, having the government forbid anyone else to sell you a car that might be more fuel efficient. In addition, the same Detroit company would make all the spare parts, and you couldn't buy them from anyone else, or even install the parts yourself once you bought them.

This time, the government's case was powerful. After one full year of the most dramatic antitrust trial in history, AT&T looked like it was going to lose. Evidence of illegal action appeared everywhere. Even AT&T employees blew the whistle on Ma Bell. So in January 1982, eight years after the case was filed, AT&T agreed to divest itself of its local phone companies if Justice would drop the case. That means that as of January 1984, AT&T and its local Bell telephone companies are separate—forever. Period. As part of the deal, AT&T gets to keep Western Electric and Bell Labs.

Under the AT&T-Justice Department agreement, AT&T had options on how it would "spin off" the local companies. It decided to divide them up into seven independent companies. Of course, consumers served by the traditional independent telephone companies will continue to be so served. All of this still affects you, though, as you'll see later.

You may have heard the phrase "telephone deregulation." This means that as more and more companies want to get into the phone business, the less and less it will be treated like a government-regulated utility. The government will control it less and marketplace forces will take over. That's true for telephone equipment, domestic long distance services, international services, and even local telephone service.

Buying phone service and phone equipment is now like shopping for almost any other product or service: cars, toasters, fishing rods, insurance, stereo gear, shoes, bank services, TVs, barbers, bicycles, and all the rest. You shop around and buy from those who give you the best price and service.

It's a whole new ballgame.

PUT YOUR MONEY WHERE YOUR MOUTH IS

Psssst. Wanna buy some cheap long distance phone service? Although you won't find a man with a smelly cigar and a bulging trenchcoat standing on the corner offering cut-rate phone service, the long distance market is becoming highly competitive with companies begging for your business.

Moreover, with the government-mandated divestiture or break-up of AT&T, you will be forced to choose a long distance company to do business with. You no longer will automatically get AT&T Long Lines, the company's long distance service, when you dial an out-of-town number.

In addition, you may receive two separate bills each month: one from your local telephone company for your basic service and local calls and another from a long distance company for long distance calls. According to the AT&T divestiture agreement, local Bell telephone companies may continue to bill you for AT&T long distance service. However, if they do, they must also bill you for service from other long distance companies you use. They can't play favorites.

The long distance company you eventually pick may or may not be AT&T. It's your choice. Competition puts you in the driver's seat, and good deals abound, if you know where to look.

More than 200 competitors offer long distance phone service. How do they do it? Two ways: either by setting up their own long distance network using microwave towers to hip-hop your call around the country (some even use satellites) or by leasing AT&T's own long distance lines in bulk and selling those lines to individual users at a cut rate.

The largest non-AT&T long distance network is MCI Communications. You've probably seen the ads: "You're not talking too much, you're just paying too much." Well, MCI and others certainly give you something to talk about. Here's how it all works:

Let's say you're in New York and want to call a friend in San Francisco. You pick up the phone and dial the local MCI switching station, a regular local phone number. After you hear a special tone, you punch in a code number that identifies you as an MCI customer. Then, you dial your friend's number—area code and seven-digit number, just like you've always done. The call is routed through MCI's network of microwave stations, which relays your call from station to station across the country until it reaches an MCI local station in San Francisco. The call then is fed back into the local San Francisco phone system for completion. AT&T Long Lines is cut out of the action.

MCI and others are able to offer you a discount over AT&T for several reasons. Ma Bell says that the cost of a long distance call has been kept intentionally high to help finance its extensive and expensive local phone system. It cost AT&T billions of dollars to establish the national network, they say, and they want to make a decent return on their investment.

But competitors argue that AT&T hasn't used the most economical technology available to build its network. AT&T could have kept the prices of long distance calls down, the argument goes, but didn't because they received guaranteed income (because they were a government-sanctioned monopoly) and didn't have to be competitive. All this bickering is academic, however. With AT&T free of its local companies, it must compete on an equal footing for long distance business. More on that later.

Long distance companies known as "resellers" offer a new twist on the business adage "buy low, sell high." For many years, AT&T has offered WATS (Wide Area Telephone Service) to large companies that make a lot of long distance calls. What AT&T actually does is lease one of its long distance lines for a flat monthly fee, a fee that is less than if the customer were to make all its long distance calls by direct dialing. Think of it as a discount for buying in bulk, just like getting a better buy per ounce of tomato sauce when you purchase the twelve-ounce can rather than the six-ounce can. With WATS, however, no matter how many calls you make, up to a prescribed hourly limit, your monthly long distance bill remains the same.

For years, WATS was the only discount phone service available

Calling Long Distance Without Ma Bell

When you call long distance using a discount company, your call often bypasses the Bell long distance network. When you dial the local access number in City A, the company's computer sends the call via its microwave network to its computer in City B. Then, the call is routed to a local switching office and via City B's local phone network to the phone you're calling.

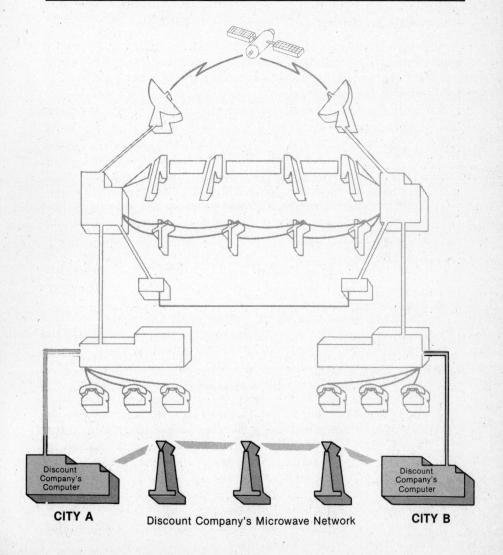

CITY A

Discount Company's Microwave Network

CITY B

until one WATS user got a bright idea. What about smaller companies that didn't make enough long distance calls to warrant getting their own WATS lines? What if a large WATS customer could sell part of its WATS line to someone else? In effect, it meant becoming a reseller of AT&T long distance service.

The idea spread like crazy. Now, companies exist just to sell you part of their WATS lines. The more WATS lines they buy from AT&T, the less they pay, and the cheaper they resell the service to you and still make a profit.

Choosing a Long Distance Company

As a consumer, you shouldn't care how the discount company sends your call—whether it's a reseller, operates its own network, or even combines the two—as long is it does what you want it to do at the cheapest rate.

For residential and small business service, the five major long distance discounters deserve the first look. They offer discounts that are up to 60 percent less than the cost of direct dialing through AT&T. Here's a brief look at each company:

- MCI: Started in 1968, MCI was the first major consumer-oriented long distance discount service. The company has more than 500 microwave towers, and its long distance network is second only to AT&T's. It has more than a million customers. Callers may be located in more than 200 metropolitan areas, and MCI can connect you with almost anyone else in the country. The company offers up to 50 percent savings over AT&T. The service features "redial": If you make an error while dialing, simply press the "#" button and begin again. No need to hang up. If you make an error while dialing your authorization code, press the "#" button and you need only redial your code, not the MCI local number. There is a minimum charge for business users, but MCI offers a "super saver account" for residential customers who only call during off hours—that is, after 5 PM weekdays, or on weekends or holidays. Service can begin in two to ten days after you sign up. Through an agreement with American Express, you can pay for MCI service on your American Express card bill as well as receive an extra 20 percent discount by enrolling through American Express.
- International Telephone & Telegraph (ITT): This company, a veteran of the international communications scene, also

Miles of Overhead Telephone Wire

Texas	144,257	Nevada	24,900
California	133,642	Maryland	23,936
New York	84,434	South Carolina	22,656
Virginia	72,265	Florida	21,497
Georgia	71,318	Mississippi	18,752
Ohio	64,383	Wyoming	17,974
Oklahoma	63,275	Massachusetts	17,365
Montana	61,031	Utah	17,343
Tennessee	57,728	Vermont	16,091
North Carolina	57,000	Wisconsin	15,320
Colorado	54,952	Maine	14,144
Pennsylvania	53,986	West Virginia	13,451
Missouri	47,904	Connecticut	13,294
Kansas	47,472	New Hampshire	12,699
Arizona	45,096	Illinois	9,061
New Mexico	43,778	Minnesota	8,509
Washington	41,843	Iowa	7,219
Oregon	41,801	Hawaii	6,980
Arkansas	35,896	South Dakota	5,773
Michigan	32,496	Nebraska	4,665
New Jersey	30,842	Louisiana	3,155
Idaho	29,827	Rhode Island	2,672
Alabama	27,336	Alaska	1,393
Kentucky	26,682	North Dakota	1,135
Indiana	25,410	Delaware	846

uses its own microwave network, which stretches from New York through Atlanta to Texas as the backbone for its "Longer Distance Service." For the rest of the country, ITT leases AT&T lines. Longer Distance is offered through ITT's company, U.S. Transmission Systems Inc., and callers may be located in more than 125 metropolitan areas. They charge a monthly fee plus a start-up charge. As with MCI, this service includes a redial feature. ITT's business service is called "ITT-USA" with special discounts for very high usage.

- Sprint: Sprint was begun by Southern Pacific Railroad, which expanded the private microwave network it used for its railroad business. Callers may be located in 250 metropolitan areas. There is a monthly fee and minimum usage charge for business customers. Sprint is the second biggest discount long distance company, just behind MCI. A unique feature is IN-Sprint: If you dial a six-digit code number from any city on the network, the call will be completed at no cost to the dialer; the IN-Sprint code holder is charged for the call. It's similar to toll-free "800" numbers. The company was bought (pending government approval) in 1982 by GTE, known formerly as General Telephone and Telegraph.

- Western Union: "Metrofone" features both a business and a residential service. The business service is in effect from 7 AM to 6 PM seven days a week. It offers several different payment plans; some require minimum usages and some don't. Western Union also offers bulk discounts to areas you often call. Residential service offers special evening and night discounts in addition to a minimum monthly usage charge. There are no start-up fees.
- Satellite Business Systems: SBS is a partnership of IBM, Aetna Life & Casualty, and Communications Satellite Corporation. It's the newest major company to establish residential and small-business long distance service. Called "SBS Skyline," it uses SBS's own three-satellite network. (Its third satellite was the first commercial payload ever sent up on the Space Shuttle.) The service was initially limited to about 20 cities, but is expected to expand quickly. Callers may call anywhere even if it's not on the SBS network. Special weekend, evening, and late-night rates are offered.

As you can see, each company offers basically the same service, but with different rates and features. All give you special code numbers that identify you as a user (it tells them where to send the bill) and most require that you use a Touch-Tone phone. Some people find pressing all those buttons a chore, but there is help. You can purchase devices that will call the discounter's office and punch in your authorization code with the touch of one button. (See Chapter Four for details.) Some discounters charge an initial fee and/or a monthly fee and some don't. Some allow calls away from your home area (a good feature if you travel a lot) and some don't. Some reach all areas of the country and some handle only major metropolitan areas. Some give a discount for off hours calling and some don't. You get the picture.

Choosing a company to suit your needs and budget isn't easy. It will require some legwork. Call each company and ask for its brochure. Then study. The above guide is only approximate because competition is getting stiffer all the time and features are being added continuously to woo customers. Prices are go-

Two Tones Are Better Than One

When you use your Touch-Tone phone, you may think you're hearing only one tone each time you press a button, but you're wrong; it's two. Picture your Touch-Tone dial as having a heading across the top of the "1," "2" and "3" saying "High Tones," and a heading down the left from the "1" to the "*" saying "Low Tones." Each "across" and "down" line is assigned one special tone from each high or low group. When you press, for example, the "8" button you're combining one high tone coming down from the "2" line and one low tone coming across from the "7" line. Because both tones need time to mix into the one that is sent over the line, the button must be pressed for at least two-tenths of a second or your call won't go through. It's common for people in a hurry to dial faster than a Touch-Tone dial can take it. Whereas, in a rotary dial, a built-in mechanical gizmo prevents the dial from rotating back faster than the circuits can read the number.

ing down, too, and start-up fees are often waived during special promotion periods to drum up more customers. The time spent investigating the various companies is worth it because choosing the right service could save you hundreds of dollars a year.

For quick comparisons, all the companies' brochures give examples of how much a call will cost from such-and-such-a-place to thus-and-thus-a-place. If you live in such-and-such and call thus-and-thus, comparison is easy. If not, you'll have to ask a salesperson for the cost between your city and the cities you call most and at the time of day you make those calls. Generally, companies don't like to have to make such comparisons because it means a lot of work for them, but it's the only way you can compare and save. If you're a large phone user, some companies will take one of your recent phone bills and show you how much you would save with their service.

There are other considerations besides price, of course. For one thing, companies that lease lines from AT&T usually have better voice quality than others; some microwave telephone networks create a disturbing echo in the phone lines or simply aren't as clear as AT&T's network. Unfortunately, the only way you will ever know is to try a service. If transmission quality is too poor for you, get rid of it and try another.

When considering resellers for your long distance service, note that most are local companies and can only carry your calls from that city. For example, at the present time, Telecommunications

Services Corporation, in Brookfield, Wisconsin, only handles calls originating in the Brookfield-Milwaukee area even though they can complete your call to anywhere in the U.S.

Some long distance companies allow you to call from any city in which they maintain a switching office. They supply you with a special travel code number that you can use away from home. You just call the local discounter's office in the area you are in and punch up your regular code number or a special travel code number. The travel number is great if you have an out-of-town college student in the family: He or she can call home, using your travel code, and you receive the bill.

All long distance companies supply itemized bills. Check their accuracy. In the past, some have been less than reliable. If a call is wrong, notify the company immediately.

Remember, AT&T is still in the long distance business with an excellent list of features and a reliable service record, but unless you relish paying top dollar, shop around.

Intrastate Long Distance Discounts

Federal law governs long distance discounters and allows them to offer services that cross state lines. But they may not offer discounts for calls originating and ending within the same state. "Intrastate" calls come under each state's jurisdiction and, until recently, most states prohibited intrastate discounters. Even if you call to the other side of your state, and it is a bona fide long distance call, you cannot get intrastate discount service unless you live in New York, Texas, Florida, or a handful of other states. Congress could eventually end restrictions in all states.

Florida, for example, once had one of the most expensive long distance rate schedules for calls within the state. But the state government gave a company called Microtel Inc. of Tampa approval to build the nation's first privately-owned statewide phone system to compete with AT&T.

In Texas, U.S. Telephone Communications of Dallas runs a discount phone service that already reaches more than 225 cities in Texas where customers once paid full long distance rates to dial across the largest state in the lower 48. They are a reseller. To find out if your state allows intrastate long distance discount services, contact your public utility commission. Many states are changing the rules in the consumer's favor.

Local Discount Services

Sorry, there are none. Not yet anyway and, unfortunately, local rates may go up before they come down. Very soon, local phone companies will tack on a special fee to your local phone bill known as an "access charge."

In the past, AT&T's long distance rates also paid part of the cost of local phone service. In fact, local service has never fully paid for itself. Now, with AT&T long distance being separated from the local Bell companies, the local companies are in a jam. They won't get subsidization from long distance calls anymore. So the FCC decided, once and for all, to let local service rates reflect their real costs. In other words, your rates will go up because they've been underpriced all along.

The new local access charge will run between $2 and $10 a month and will be phased in over several years so you'll hardly feel the initial pinch. You'll not only be paying for the use of the local lines but also for the privilege of connecting to the various long distance services.

Of course, even if you don't make any long distance calls you will be charged for long distance access. It's kind of like paying school taxes even if you don't have any school-aged children or road taxes even if you don't drive.

But every cloud has a silver lining. With the access charge and the AT&T divestiture came the rule that a local phone company must give equal interconnection access to all long distance phone companies—AT&T, MCI, Sprint, and all the rest. So far, a nationwide numbering plan hasn't been worked out, but probably you'll dial 4 additional digits—not one—for long distance service: 1111 for AT&T, 1112 for MCI, 1113 for ITT, and so on before dialing the area code and number.

That's the good news. Here's the bad news:

Right now, you can get unlimited local service in most areas—you make as many calls as you want for a single monthly fee—but local companies are moving towards what they call "local measured service," where you pay for the time you talk even if it's only next door. That includes time spent on long distance calls as well: When you call AT&T, MCI, or anyone else to make a five-minute long distance call, you'll be making a five-minute local call at the same time. You'll be billed for the call by both your local phone company *and* your long distance phone company.

That could get expensive, so in order to lessen the sting of local measured service, local companies may soon offer you the chance to use the cheapest long distance service for any particular call. It's done by an ingenious scheme known as "least-cost routing." For a small fee or no fee at all, the local phone company connects you to the best long distance deal for the call you are making. You press, say, the numbers "1100," and the telephone company scans its computer banks, comparing all the available long distance companies' rates for that time of day and distance and automatically connects you with the cheapest one.

To make things even easier, least-cost routing lets your local phone company handle the billing for all of the long distance carriers (on an equal basis, of course; no favorites allowed) so you pay for it all on your regular local phone bill, all itemized, just like it is now. All this is a good idea, but it will take a few years to implement it nationwide.

It is starting, however. Near Houston, for example, the Sugar Land Telephone Company offers its 37,000 customers least-cost routing between MCI and AT&T. When a signed-up customer dials a long distance number, the call is automatically routed to the less costly of the two long distance companies. Until all local phone companies offer least-cost routing, though, discount long

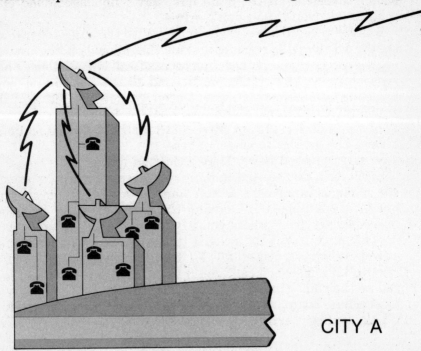

CITY A

distance services that you subscribe to by yourself are the only way to go.

There are some dangers in the new local access charges. To many phone users, these charges may be so expensive that they will discontinue phone service. Ironically, this will affect primarily the poor, who won't be able to afford their telephone service anymore, and very large companies, which won't be able to afford to pay access charges on each line because they have so many lines coming into their offices.

First, the poor. They probably will be eligible for so-called "lifeline service," a basic phone service for a modest fee. It would allow them to use their present phone for emergencies, like calling the police, fire department, or doctor. No long distance calls allowed.

Now, for the large companies. Because they have so much telephone traffic, they might decide to bypass the local phone system and connect their phones directly to a long distance company via private lines. They can do this in several ways. One method is to use cable TV. (MCI is experimenting with this.) Right now, cable passes more than a third of American homes and businesses. Hooking into the cable has technical problems, but they can be worked out.

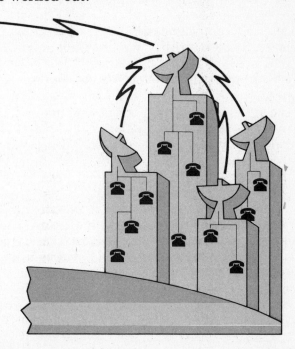

CITY B

The other method carries the fancy moniker of "digital termina-tion systems." DTS are composed of many microwave dishes placed atop buildings. All the telephones in those buildings are connected to the roof dishes by special wires or fiber optic lines through the walls. Fiber optic cables take the place of regular wire cables. Instead of using electrical energy to carry your voice, it uses minute light beams. The advantage of fiber cables is that they can carry many more conversations than metal cables, and they are less prone to "cross-talk," that annoying phenomenon where you hear another phone conversation faintly during your call. (See box, page 41.)

The dishes atop all these buildings relay their messages to one central dish on the tallest building in town. There, the messages are sent up to a satellite and relayed back down to earth in another city with a similar DTS network. The local phone company and AT&T Long Lines are cut out of the action. For a large company, it's cheaper than using the local phone network. In addition, DTS handles very high speed data (regular telephone wires can't do that) and businesses send a lot of information at high speeds by computer. Banks and insurance companies in particular transmit bucketloads of numbers that must be sent quickly.

In New York City, for example, the Port Authority of New York and New Jersey is constructing a "Teleport" on Staten Island that will accept signals directly from large Wall Street companies and send them directly via hovering satellites to thousands of companies and individuals. It's not DTS—the signals will travel by fiber optic cables instead of microwaves—but the result is the same: bypassing the local phone company.

Now, that isn't all bad except that in most cities the large com-panies pay a lot of money to the local phone companies for their service. If that huge cache of money disappears, other users must take up the slack. That's right, buckaroos, the residential and small-business user faces higher local service charges if this bypassing stuff catches on.

In Las Vegas, for instance, it is catching on. Many casinos bypass the local phone company and go directly to a long distance company via microwave towers placed atop the casinos. And the local phone patrons face higher rates because of it. All this can be avoided, however, if the access charge is kept low enough so bypassing isn't worthwhile. It's clear that local phone companies must install new equipment, like DTS and fiber optic cables, to accept high speed data and remain competitive.

Telephone Ownership, by State
(Phones per 100 residents)

District of Columbia	167.33	Rhode Island	76.71
Nevada	103.10	Minnesota	76.69
Illinois	89.92	Montana	76.36
Delaware	89.31	Indiana	76.30
New Jersey	88.84	Idaho	75.22
California	88.00	South Dakota	75.09
Florida	86.36	Hawaii	74.66
North Dakota	85.50	Ohio	74.66
Connecticut	85.14	Utah	74.56
Maryland	84.73	New York	73.78
Pennsylvania	83.12	Wisconsin	73.60
Colorado	82.55	Virginia	73.38
Nebraska	82.31	North Carolina	73.01
Kansas	80.72	Vermont	73.00
Wyoming	80.40	Tennessee	72.42
Washington	79.89	Maine	72.03
Oklahoma	79.73	Louisiana	71.30
Texas	79.67	South Carolina	70.44
Georgia	79.55	New Mexico	68.65
Arizona	79.17	Alabama	66.72
Massachusetts	78.89	Arkansas	65.66
Michigan	78.52	Kentucky	64.93
Iowa	78.49	Alaska	64.36
New Hampshire	78.22	Mississippi	62.97
Missouri	77.85	West Virginia	59.24
Oregon	77.73		

So, where does all this heady stuff leave us? In the long run, local phone service costs will go up but long distance service costs will go down. How much, nobody really knows. Stay tuned.

International Discounts

There are none now, but there will be very soon, thanks to new-found competition.

Since the 1930s, international communications has been divided into two groups of users: those who sent voice and those who sent data. The voice part was left to AT&T and the data part was left to companies known as "international record carriers." IRCs were permitted only to handle stuff like Telex, telegrams, and cables. In other words, printed records and the like. That's why they're called "record carriers." (More on Telex and IRCs in Chapter Three.) IRCs were restricted to international service and not allowed to send messages within the U.S. At the same time, AT&T was not allowed to send data overseas.

The situation changed in 1982, when the FCC opened the door for any communications company to do practically anything. Now, IRCs such as RCA Global Communications, Western Union International, and ITT can, for the first time, engage in domestic voice and data traffic. (Remember ITT's long distance discount service?) And AT&T can send data overseas.

MCI, for example, began discount phone service to Canada in early 1983, and is expected to expand it to Europe. Other companies will follow suit.

So, while AT&T is still the big wheel for overseas calls, that won't remain the case, and calling your aunt across the ocean will soon be as cheap as calling your uncle across the country.

TEACHING YOUR OLD PHONE NEW TRICKS

The game is called "telephone tag." But unlike other tag games this isn't much fun. You call someone who isn't in and leave a message. They call back and you're not around. And on and on. Surveys show that 70 percent of all telephone calls go uncompleted on the first try.

To eliminate telephone tag, companies looked to the Postal Service for inspiration. As you probably know, if you're away from your home or office, on vacation perhaps, the post office will hold your mail and not deliver it until you get back. Or, they may forward your mail to where you're vacationing. Well, now you can do that and more for telephone calls with a service known variously as "voice store and forward" or "voice mail."

To leave a message for someone, you dial a special number and a computerized voice asks you for the recipient's phone number. You punch that in on your Touch-Tone telephone. Then the voice asks when you want the message delivered. You respond by punching up the date and time. Some systems allow you to leave a message that will be delivered up to 30 days later. Then, the computer voice asks you to give your message. You clear your throat and begin, recording a message up to a half-hour long. When you finish, you can have it played back and even edit it if necessary. The computer stores your voice, rings the recipient's phone at the designated time, and forwards your recorded message.

That's the basic idea, but most voice mail systems allow you to do much more. For example, you can send your message to many people at once, or the same message to many people at different times. All in your own voice. (Any murder mystery writers out there see some story possibilities?)

Voice mail systems even let users set up computerized storage bins that keep calls until asked for. Suppose you don't want to be disturbed all morning. No problem; any calls left for you get held by the computer. Later, after lunch perhaps, you call the computer and receive them. You can even ask the computer for a list of those who called and listen to their messages in any order you desire. It's sort of like looking through your mail and picking out the ones you want to open first.

With voice mail, two people could conceivably carry on a conversation over the phone even when both of them were elsewhere.

The possibilities seem endless. Got a telephone conference scheduled for next Thursday? For the asking, the computer will check with all the parties at the agreed-upon time. If some lines are busy, it will wait and not ring anyone until all are free to talk. Then it will call everyone on the list and connect them.

Voice mail doesn't come cheap, however. A complete system for your office starts around $50,000. That's not too bad for a large company; it could clock in at only $200 to $500 per user. But for the small businessperson or consumer, there are other ways to get voice mail without spending a fortune.

Some local telephone companies offer voice mail as part of their "custom-calling" services. Instead of installing the computer in your office, it is kept at the main telephone office and is used by all telephone customers who want it.

If your local telephone company doesn't yet offer voice mail, you can still get it by contacting a non-telephone-company voice mail firm offering it in your area as dial-up service. You simply call their voice mail computer for the price of a local call. If they are located far away, they may have a toll-free number. Most companies charge a monthly fee plus any long distance charges for their voice mail service.

Along with voice mail, the computer can handle other less-exotic jobs such as "call forwarding." If you will be at another number, just tell the computer where you can be reached. Your calls automatically will be forwarded. The computer can also divert incoming calls to your pocket pager so you'll never be out of touch. (See Chapter Six for more on pagers.)

The computer can also give you "call waiting." If you are on the phone, and someone tries to call you, you hear a soft beep. You excuse yourself, depress the phone receiver and talk to

Sorry, The Li-on Is Busy

There is more than one kind of busy signal. The one most often heard is slow and even—about one second on and one second off; dial your own number to hear what it sounds like. The other busy signal is more rapid and sometimes louder. It indicates that the large-capacity "trunk" lines serving a major area are tied up. You may hear that sound on Mother's Day, when more long distance calls are made than during any other day of the year. (Actually, it barely surpasses Christmas Day as the year's busiest telephone day.) When you hear the rapid busy signal, try your call again soon. Trunk lines rarely stay filled up for long.

whomever is calling you. You can then tell this second caller to wait while you take care of the first caller, or you can say you'll call back. Then, you depress the hook to get back to the original call. You can keep switching back and forth as long as neither caller hangs up.

So much for the good news.

Although voice mail and related services mimic the good side of conventional mail, they also mimic the worst part: junk mail. That's right. With a voice mail computer, a company can call you and millions of others with junk voice mail messages to buy this, that, and the other thing. Or, it could ask you what program you're watching, what you're eating, or for whom you're casting your vote for president. Some states prohibit such calls, but if your state doesn't you are left to your own devious devices. Perhaps you'd like a telephone that rejects all calls except from those using a secret code number, which only you and those you want to call know? That's available. (See Chapter Four.) Or, you can always counter the junk voice mail caller with your own recorded message: "Return to Sender!"

How to Call a Typewriter

Suppose you had to get in touch with someone in China, Mozambique, or Qatar. What would you do? You could try direct dialing, but right now these countries aren't hooked up for that. Or you could try dialing with operator assistance, but even if you got through, what happens if the operator on the other end doesn't speak English? How would you communicate?

Okay, so you'll never need to contact anyone in China, Mozam-

bique, or Qatar. But how about England, Germany, or
Switzerland? Suppose you wanted to buy a Swiss watch from a
company in Bern. How would you do it?

The answer is Telex, a domestic and international network that
melds the best parts of the telephone and the typewriter. More
than a million companies and individuals, especially those who
deal internationally, use Telex. The beauty of Telex is that it's
cheap—much less than calling by phone—and the best part is that
you can leave a written message. It's perfect for ordering that
watch when it's midday in the U.S. but after business hours in
Bern.

And for some countries, Telex remains the only reliable electronic link to the rest of the world.

Simply put, a Telex machine is a typewriter with a built-in
telephone. Instead of talking into the machine, you type your
message. To send it, you press a special button to send your
message to the company that will transmit it overseas. You get
a message back saying "go-ahead," and you dial the Telex number
of the country you're calling and the number of the receiving
party. Once connected, you get an "answerback" message iden-
tifying the receiving party. For example, the FCC's Gettysburg,
Pennsylvania, Telex machine answers "FEDCOMCOMM GBG."
That obviously stands for "Federal Communications Commission,
Gettysburg." Then, you send your message. Your message is
printed out on a paper roll, even if no one is actually at the receiving terminal.

Companies that specialize as middlemen for international Telex
messages are the same international record carriers referred to
in Chapter Two. They are called "record carriers" because they
handle records or printed matter but (until recently) not voice.
An IRC contracts with your local phone company to install a
special phone line connecting your machine with its office. The
largest domestic Telex company is Western Union and the largest
international Telex operators are ITT, RCA, and Western Union
International.

If you don't have your own Telex machine, don't despair. Just
bring your message to a local IRC office, and they will type it
and send it. Rates vary according to how long it takes to send
the message and where it's going. A 60-word message from the
U.S. to England, for example, costs about a dollar. As with a
telegram, it's cheaper to send a "night Telex," which is transmitted during a time when the phone rates are lower.

Making Things Perfectly Clear

The phone company calls it "crosstalk," but you probably call it annoying. Crosstalk is when you hear another conversation on your line. It's caused when electrical fields from one pair of telephone wires carrying one conversation are absorbed by a nearby pair of wires that happen to be carrying your conversation. Because of the differences in those fields, you may be able to hear the other conversation, but they may not be able to hear yours.

According to the law, the phone company must eliminate crosstalk to comply with privacy laws. However, in most cases, crosstalk is a random occurrence and almost impossible to find. If crosstalk makes your conversation impossible, hang up and immediately call the operator for credit and a new connection. If crosstalk is chronic, call the phone company's repair service for a permanent fix. Often, a technician need only reroute your line or replace it with one shielded by a metal casing.

Many IRCs offer extra services. For companies that send a lot of overseas messages, IRCs will bill you at the end of the month with all charges neatly laid out and itemized. And some offer "broadcast" services in which the same message is sent automatically to different offices. It's ideal for companies with branches around the world.

Also, IRCs can send your Telex message to anyone in the U.S. who has a Telex machine. For many small companies, it's a convenient and inexpensive way to send orders to suppliers because the recipient gets a written requisition.

In addition, some IRCs combine high-technology Telex with low-technology messengers. If your message is going to a remote part of a country where there is no Telex machine, the printed message from the nearest Telex machine will be dispatched by messenger or mail, similar to the once-common telegram, which has all but faded from the American scene because of readily accessible long distance telephone service.

Another service you may have heard about is TWX, pronounced "twicks." This is shorthand for Teletypewriter Exchange. A TWX machine looks very much like a Telex machine except that it runs faster (about 100 words per minute compared with 66 for Telex) and can be used for two-way written "conversations" using the keyboard.

More important, TWX works on the regular telephone network. You don't need to have a special telephone line installed. You simply dial the TWX number of the recipient, and when someone answers you begin sending your message. Or, if you want, you can leave a message on an unattended machine. You can use TWX for overseas calls, too.

Nothing But the Fax

Before he allegedly shot his facsimile machine full of holes, Hunter S. Thompson, the self-proclaimed dean of "gonzo journalism," is said to have fed it with pages of a small Colorado town telephone book. He allegedly did this because an anxious editor demanded an overdue story the intrepid reporter had not yet written. "Chew on that for a while," shouted Thompson as the hungry facsimile machine turned and turned, transmitting the local phone book's gibberish over the phone lines. But then, prompted by the angry faraway editor, the machine buzzed again for some *real* copy. Thompson promptly put the machine out of its misery with some well-placed shots from a .357 Magnum.

Despite Thompson's disdain for the lowly facsimile machine, most businesses don't share his disrespect. More than 400 million pages a year are sent by facsimile machines—"fax," as they're commonly called—more than any other form of electronic mail. A common office brand is "Qwip," a product of Exxon.

Fax isn't new. It dates back to the 1930s but fell out of favor because of its slow speed. It could take more than six minutes to transmit or receive a full page. As telephone rates rose, six minutes on the hook became expensive. In addition, the quality was lousy. Pictures lost their detail and printed words looked like they were smeared while the ink was drying.

However, new high-speed, high-quality facsimile machines are making their way back into users' good graces. The main advantage is that they're simple to use. Just place the page you want sent onto the fax's drum, close the cover, dial the recipient's telephone number, and press the button. As the machine scans the copy, it sends the image bit by bit over the phone lines to the recipient's fax. The new machines send near-perfect images of a document in less than a minute. Drawings, certificates, maps, newspaper clippings, graphs, even photos come out almost exact. It's especially useful when you need to send a signature or blueprint.

The secret to good quality is in the number of lines per inch. Look closely at your TV set; pictures are formed by lines of varying color shades. If there were more lines per inch, you could get

---

First Facts

Alexander Graham Bell generally is credited with inventing and publicly demonstrating the first, workable telephone, but the first device capable of sending speech over wires was built by Italian-born Antonio Meucci in Havana, Cuba, in 1849. He was too poor to file a patent, but he was able to borrow $20 and file a caveat (a letter preceding a patent request) in 1871. The instrument was never publicly demonstrated but it worked, according to the caveat, albeit poorly.

Ironically, the first words ever spoken clearly over the telephone were unintentional. Bell and his assistant, Thomas A. Watson, set up an experimental phone between two rooms in Bell's house in Boston. While trying different substances to conduct electricity in the mouthpiece, Bell would talk into the device while Watson listened to the receiver.

During some experiments on March 10, 1876, Bell accidentally spilled acid on his pants and shouted in pain: "Watson, come here I want you." Watson heard the call through the receiver and rushed to help his suffering boss who expressed amazement that the thing really worked as well as it did.

---

greater detail. The same with fax: the more lines, the greater the detail. The latest machines employ hundreds of lines per page.

Unlike many older machines, new faxes "print" images with laser beams. In fact, most newspapers use laser faxes to send photos to and from their field photographers, as well as to receive copy from reporters.

The best thing about fax is that it's universal. Although there are exceptions, most fax machines will work with any other fax machine. An average fax machine costs anywhere from several hundred dollars to more than $10,000 for super-deluxe models that let you send and receive text to and from computers and Telex machines as well as other faxes.

But even if you don't own a fax machine, you can send your pages via fax. Western Union International, for example, maintains a Facsimile Bureau Service that accepts your document by mail or over the counter in New York, San Francisco, Washington, D.C., Miami, and New Orleans. From there, the company sends it to any fax machine in the world. If the recipient doesn't have a machine, the fax-equipped WUI bureau overseas will deliver the document by mail or messenger, or you can have it picked up.

Even the Postal Service offers a similar service called Intelepost. Many post offices around the country will accept your document in person and perform almost the same service. One page costs about $5 and more than a half-dozen countries including England, Canada, and Germany have joined the Intelepost network.

Anything-to-Anything Networks

Your sixth-grade math teacher probably told you that you can't add apples and oranges because they're different fruits. But while that may be true for fruits, it's not true for communications devices.

Telephone networks now exist that allow you to mix all different kinds of communications devices so that they can "talk" to each other. Usually, a Telex machine can only talk with another Telex machine, and a fax machine can only send and receive with another fax machine, but the new breed of anything-to-anything networks is changing all that. They act as interpreters and mixers for the different machines and their unique languages, and can send your message anywhere in the world.

One such system is called "Freedom Network," from Graphnet

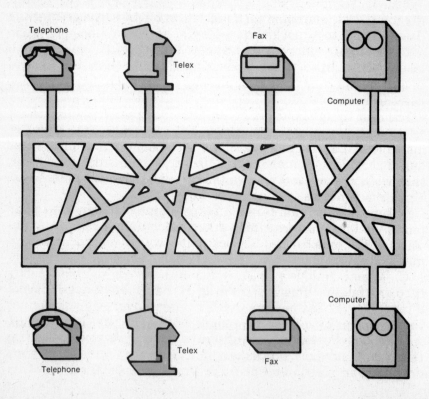

Inc. By calling the network on your phone, you can connect your home computer to any other computer, even if it is made by a different company and uses a different format. Or, you can connect your computer to an overseas Telex machine. Or, connect your Telex machine to someone else's fax machine. You can even arrange to have the network print out a letter written on your word processor and deliver it by hand in a foreign country.

The charge to use Freedom Network is only $5 per month when you tap into the network through your phone line, plus whatever costs are accrued in the transmission of your message. Costs range from 28 to 43 cents per minute, depending upon the equipment used and its speed. There are additional charges for international messages costing from just over $1 per minute to England to around $3 per minute to Africa.

Freedom Network also offers store-and-forward services plus other computer-enhanced goodies.

ITT offers a service they call "FAXPAK." Although originally designed to connect dissimilar model fax machines, it now can interconnect other types of machines through ITT's "World Com" network. You don't need special equipment—other than a fax, Telex, TWX, or computer, that is—just a Touch-Tone telephone. You get access to FAXPAK by dialing a local phone number or ITT's toll-free "800" number. Then you send the message to their computer and it does the rest. You can send from a Telex to a TWX, a word processor to a Telex, a fax machine to a word processor, or any combination you want. FAXPAK also offers a store-and-forward service.

Western Union International also has an anything-to-anything network called "Easy Link." And companies like GTE Telenet and Tymnet also permit connections of some dissimilar computers and word processors through the telephone network, but not on such a wide scale for the small user.

The best way to shop for these services is to determine what you need and then see who has it. There is no use in paying for a network that has more capability than you can use. Why pay for a Rolls Royce when a Toyota will do nicely?

Dial the World

Many local telephone companies and almost all Bell telephone companies offer direct international dialing to about 90 countries. To dial direct you must know the country code (a two- or three-digit number); the city code (a one- to five-digit number); and the local phone number. You also need a Touch-Tone phone, by the way. Simply dial the international access code (011) + the country code + the city code (sometimes it's not required) + the local phone number + the # symbol next to the "0" on your telephone. The "#," for some magical reason, speeds the call. Without it, your call could take 45 seconds to get through. With it, expect to be connected in less than 10 seconds.

So, for a call to Buckingham Palace, dial 011 + 44 + 1 + 930-4832 + #. Say hello to the Queen, or to Princess Di. Or try calling 011 + 81 + 3 + 503-2911 for the latest recorded events in Tokyo. (It's in English, but if you want the French version dial 503-2926.) For home cooking, British style, try 011 + 44 + 1 + 246-8071 for "Recipeline." You can get the weather in Bangkok by calling 011 + 66 + 2 + 392-9000, but unless you speak Thai, you're wasting your money. And don't forget the "#" for all of these. Without it, you'll wait longer than you have to.

Even if your area doesn't have direct international dialing and requires operator assistance you will be charged the same rate as those whose areas do. However, credit card, collect, or person-to-person calls cost more. Be sure to dial the international access code (011) quickly, or the telephone will only read the first "0" and you will get the local operator instead of your distant party. AT&T maintains a toll-free number to answer questions about international dialing: 800-874-4000.

So far, AT&T has the most extensive and sophisticated international phone service, and until recently it was the only company allowed to offer it. Other companies are beginning to enter the international phone business because of recently relaxed restrictions.

WATS Happening

Toll-free "800" numbers are the best thing to happen to telephone consumers since Alexander Graham Bell. They allow you to call anyone who subscribes to the service at no charge; the recipient picks up the tab. Toll-free "800" numbers are a service of AT&T. If you want an "800" number for your business, it costs about $150 per line plus the cost of all incoming calls. Or, you can "rent" an "800" number from a company that maintains one and takes incoming calls for several clients.

AT&T now allows you to order special numbers to fit your

The Sky's Not The Limit

Flying to the moon on gossamer wings is child's play compared to making a phone call on the trail of a meteor. That's right, the trail of a meteor.

It has been discovered that radio waves can bounce off ionized parts of the air left by meteors as they scoot across the sky. The meteor moves so quickly that it excites the air particles in its path, charging them with electrons and leaving them acting as a mirror to radio waves. Each trail burst lasts about two-tenths of a second, but millions of such bursts happen all the time. All you have to do is find them.

That's not easy, but it's accomplished by sending hundreds of "query" signals into the sky. Once a signal is transmitted from a station in, say, Chicago, and hits a meteor trail, it is reflected back to the receiver, which can be more than 1600 miles away on Earth—Miami, for example. The receiver in Miami sends back its own signal to Chicago (via the meteor, of course) saying, in effect, "Okay, we verify the connection. Go ahead." Then the real information is sent.

All this happens in less than two-tenths of a second, mind you, so each transmission must be very high speed. Because of that restriction, computer data, so far, appears to be the best stuff to send via meteor. The Department of Agriculture uses remote meteor burst transmitters to send snowfall and rainfall information from backwoods outposts to a central station for evaluation. NATO's European forces use meteor bursts for sending top-secret messages because the signals are hard to find unless you know exactly where to look—and there are a lot of meteors out there from which to choose. Also, meteor burst transmissions are not subject to atmospheric conditions such as fading, which plague ordinary shortwave transmissions.

At least one company makes a portable meteor burst unit about three times the size of an attache case. Sending voice transmissions is still a bit dicey, but experiments continue and chances are that one day you'll be able to use one.

business. All you have to do is pick numbers that correspond to the right letters. For example, United Airlines uses 800-PACKAGE for its delivery service and National Car Rental has 800-CAR-RENT. One company will help you choose the right numbers; it has bought the rights to hundreds of combinations in the hopes of leasing them. The company's name is CIPHREX and their phone number is—you guessed it: 800-CIPHREX.

Always use "800" numbers when you can. It saves money. If you are booking hotel or airline reservations, check to see if those companies have "800" service. Several toll-free directories are on the market. However, you can find any listed number by calling the toll-free operator at 800-555-1212.

While we're on the subject of phone numbers, remember that most numbers beginning with the digits 555 aren't legitimate. Mostly, they are used by actors in TV shows when giving a phone number as part of the story. There are exceptions, however. If you want directory assistance for a city outside your local calling area, dial (area code) + 555-1212. Another exception is AT&T itself, which set up a toll-free number, 800-555-5000, to operate through most of 1984. The person on the other end will answer your questions about service, rates and anything else related to the company's divestiture.

What You See Is What You Get

In the 1960s, telephone consumers saw the future and it at once scared and delighted them. AT&T unveiled "Picturephone," a device that would allow phone users to see the party on the other end as well as hear them. Thousands of visitors to the 1964 World's Fair in New York City tried the phone/mini-TV screen combination and they either loved it or hated it immediately.

Some teenagers figured they could hold up their math homework to the camera and work on problems with friends. Businesspeople hoped it would save them hundreds of miles of air travel a year by substituting for face-to-face interviews and meetings.

But others decided that the present-day audio-only phones hid a multitude of sins such as Saturday afternoon curlers and early morning face stubble. The new-fangled gear seemed to be a Big Brother-like invasion of privacy.

Consumers never had a chance to find out what Picturephone would bring because AT&T dropped the project at the end of the

1960s when it concluded that consumers weren't willing to pay the $50-plus-a-month price tag. And businesspeople remained content with voice-only conferences by phone. Besides, technical problems plagued the original Picturephone system, and they weren't worth fixing.

Recently, however, the idea of Picturephone-like service is being resurrected, aimed more toward businesses than consumers. The service goes by the name of "video teleconferencing," or "videoconferencing" for short, and although it's in its infancy, billions of dollars are riding on its success.

Unlike early proposals of a Picturephone in every home, using a 5½-inch screen and a black-and-white TV camera staring you in the face, companies are building luxurious videoconferencing rooms, complete with wall-sized TV screens and electronic "blackboards" on which to write. The entire meeting room is included in the transmitted picture, not just "talking heads." You can rent rooms by the hour or even own them outright.

The whole idea is to save time and money. A typical business meeting may last only an hour yet it could require you to travel several hours, perhaps book a hotel room, and spend a tidy sum

on meals and cabs. When the price of gasoline and jet fuel
skyrocketed in the mid 1970s, so did interest in videoconferencing, but it wasn't until the early 1980s that the technology was
available to make it possible.

At least a half-dozen companies have established video
teleconferencing meeting rooms around the nation available for
rent. For example, Hi-Net Communications, a subsidiary of Holiday Inns, uses its satellite earth stations (it originally built them
to receive cable TV programs for hotel guests) for one-way video
teleconferencing and two-way audioconferencing. They are used
mostly for company-wide meetings, product announcements, or
press conferences. For example, a client such as 3M or TRW tells
its employees around the nation to gather at the nearest Holiday Inn (there are more than 150) for an important announcement.
The scattered employees see and hear the news directly from company executives and ask questions via telephone. Hilton hotels
have a similar service.

AT&T offers meeting rooms in 42 cities where customers can
see and talk with others in any of the other meeting rooms. Using
special devices, users can send copies of pictures and slides, even
draw images on an electronic "blackboard" that appears on the
screens of those on the other end. A typical charge to a customer
using two public rooms to conduct a one-hour meeting between
New York and Washington is about $1,300. A similar meeting
between New York and Los Angeles costs about $2,300. The com-
pany also builds and maintains private rooms for customers who
need to use them frequently.

Satellite Business Systems builds special video teleconferencing rooms on customers' premises. The comfortable, plush rooms
even include a slightly triangular table to cut down on distortion.
Ever notice how railroad tracks seem to come together in the
distance? The same thing happens to tables when viewed by a
camera sitting at the head of a long table. So, designers widened
the furthest end of the table to compensate. Smart, huh?

The tables also sport a built-in device into which you place
documents. At the press of a button, the page is electronically
sent to those on the receiving end and can show up on your own
screen as well. The other party can receive it on a screen or as
a paper copy. Each room has a master control that allows you
to control the voice volume and picture magnification. These
special digs cost about $50,000 to $100,000 and are aimed at companies with many offices who need to keep in close "personal"
contact.

More First Facts

- The first telephone for domestic use was installed in April 1877 at the home of Charles Williams, Jr.,of Somerville,Massachusetts, near Boston.

- The first telephone booth was installed by the Connecticut Telephone Company in its lobby in New Haven on June 1, 1880.

- The first coast-to-coast dial-it-yourself call was made November 10,1951, between Englewood, New Jersey, Mayor M. Leslie Denning and Alameda, California, Mayor Frank P. Osborn.

- The first international phone call was made July 1,1881, between Calais, Maine, and St. Stephen, New Brunswick.

- The first female telephone operator was Emma M. Nutt. She began work in September 1, 1878, for the Telephone Despatch Co. in Boston. Previously, all operators were men.

- The first interstate call took place May 17, 1877, between New Brunswick, New Jersey, and New York City.

- The first mobile telephone call was made September 11,1946,between a *Houston Post* newspaper reporter in Houston and one for the *St. Louis Globe Democrat* in Missouri.

- The first commercial transatlantic telephone service was established January 7, 1927, between New York City and London. The charge was $75 for three minutes.

You can even keep in video touch internationally. Intercontinental Hotels built the first international satellite video teleconferencing service available to the general public. The hotel chain began service in late 1982 between Hotel Intercontinental in New York City and one in London's Hyde Park district. The cost ranges from about $6,000 to $10,000 per hour (depending upon the time of day) and Intercontinental expects to expand the service to several more of its luxury hotels worldwide within the next several years.

Even local TV stations are getting in on the act. Several public broadcasting stations, which already have the studios and the expertise in TV broadcasting, have decided to go into video teleconferencing. There are 285 public TV stations in the U.S., all connected to the same satellite, so you could hold a teleconference between two or more such cities using their studios.

So, if plain old audio conferences just won't do it anymore, give video teleconferencing a try. At first, it may seem weird, talking to and seeing someone far away. But, through rooms designed for maximum comfort, more and more people who could never work in front of a camera are doing it. And it will have to do, of course, until three-dimensional holography becomes more developed. Then, you could have someone thousands of miles away projected by laser beam into the seat next to you.

Services for the Handicapped

For hearing-impaired phone users, several special devices are available. For example, customers can buy phones with built-in amplifiers. By turning an adjusting wheel on the handset, you can adjust the volume of the voice being received. For those with more severe hearing loss, other handset models offer additional amplification by pressing a button. On both models, the volume may be adjusted to normal levels as well. For those who use headset amplifiers, instead of models that fit into or behind the ear, small plug-in amplifiers are available. These amplifiers increase the sound before it reaches the headset.

Many phone companies also offer teletype services for deaf customers. Commonly known as TDD, for Telecommunications Device for the Deaf, these units have a typewriter keyboard and readable display or paper printer. They are similar to a teletypewriter and sometimes referred to as TTYs instead of TDDs. By hooking it to the phone, deaf people can carry on a conversation with other deaf people or with anyone else who uses a TDD. Most police and fire departments maintain a special number for emergency use by TDD users. In addition, AT&T maintains a toll-free number for inquiries via TDD. The TDD operator, at 800-855-1155, can get phone numbers for you and assist you in making long distance person-to-person calls, credit card calls, or any other service available to customers with normal hearing. In addition, TDD users may have their TDD telephone number listed in local phone books, but to protect them from heinous burglars who might take advantage of their handicap, TDD customers may omit their addresses.

To alert hearing-impaired or deaf people that someone is trying to call them, several ingenious methods are used. For those with slight impairment, an extra loud bell might do the trick. Or, a customer can buy a bell that concentrates its sound in a frequency range that the person can hear. For example, many elderly people lose their ability to hear higher-frequency sounds. For them, a gong in the bass-frequency range will work well.

The Numbers Game

In the early 1950s, AT&T began changing phone numbers from a system using two letters of an exchange name (remember BEachwood 4-5789?) to "all-number calling." Expecting public resistance, the company moved slowly, beginning in rural areas then moving to larger cities. The first major city to change over to the new all-number system was Council Bluffs, Iowa, in March 1960, with 26,000 customers taking it all in stride. But when Bell tried to change to all numbers in San Francisco, an opposing group that called itself the Anti-Digit Dialing League fought the move. In Washington, D.C., a movement dubbed the Committee of Ten Million to Oppose All-Number Calling held rallies and signed petitions. Public outrage was so fierce all over the country that AT&T, finally, in 1966 stopped changing old exchanges to the all-number system. Only new telephone installations bore all numbers; the others were left alone.

For those handicapped by complete hearing loss, a light can be rigged to indicate when a phone is ringing. An AT&T product called "Signalman" allows you to connect a lamp to a telephone. If the lamp is already on when a call is received, it flashes off at each ring; if it's off, it flashes on at each ring. "Signalman" also allows users to plug in other devices, such as an electric fan, which blows air toward a person who is both blind and deaf.

The telephone revolution won't pass by those with impaired speech, either. They can use TDD or buy handsets that amplify their voice and, if necessary, the voice at the other end of the line.

For those with poor vision, there are Touch-Tone phones with oversized buttons. They're common even in homes of people with perfect vision; some people just find them convenient. If you don't want to buy a new phone, several charities and foundations and some phone companies offer free, oversized stickers that fit over Touch-Tone buttons. There also is a rotary dial stick-on version. (Some phone companies exempt those who can't use a telephone directory because of vision problems or other handicap from paying a directory assistance charge each time they call for a number. It's worth checking into.)

One new product from AT&T permits deaf-blind customers to use the phone. The special phone converts sound into vibrations on a small disk. If the signals are coded in a special way, such as Morse code-type dots and dashes, the deaf-blind person can "read" the message by touch. For years, blind and deaf ham radio operators have carried on conversations with other hams by holding their fingers to the speakers, which vibrate with the Morse code.

Of course, those with impaired movements can use many of the new electronic phone gizmos, such as speed dialers, speaker-phones, or headset-microphone combinations. See Chapter Four for details.

THE PLAIN BLACK PHONE ISN'T PLAIN (OR BLACK) ANYMORE

In the beginning, a man with an odd assortment of tools hanging off his belt came to your home, wired the premises, called the operator to check the circuits, and left you with a shiny new telephone. The only real decisions you had to make were whether the phone should be Touch-Tone or rotary dial, or whether you should be daring and forsake the standard black model for an off-white Princess. Such decisions.

All that has changed. When the phone company representative leaves your home now, the only visible signs of his or her visit are wall jacks. (In some states, the person with the equipment belt won't even make an appearance, since you're allowed to do inside wiring yourself; more on that later.) And when you go shopping for a phone to plug in the wall, you're going to find every conceivable telephone gizmo except a phone that doubles as a food processor. (That, we suspect, will be along soon enough.)

Gone are the days of mere desk phones and simple wall models. Say hello to Bobos, Lidos, Tempos, and Kangaroos. Erica, the European pedestal model, comes in red, ivory, or mint; the Contempora, usable as either a desk or wall model, is available in white, avocado, lemonade, beige, deep blue, candy apple red, or espresso brown. There are phones that look like Pac-Man, Ronald MacDonald, Mickey Mouse, and Snoopy; country wall phones ("Hello, Jenny, get me Doc Weaver") and gold-plated French phones; cordless, collapsible, and clock-radio phones. There are phones you use on airplanes, phones you use at sea, hands-free phones, and phones that dial or redial with the push of one button. There are phones with calculators, clocks, calendars, and bulletin boards; speaker phones and amplifier phones; phones that chime, beep, light up, and call your doctor automatically.

And don't forget accessories. There are off-the-phone recording devices and on-the-phone dialing devices. There are answering machines, hold adapters, headsets, and James Bond-caliber equipment to ensure that no one is using your phone without your knowledge. There are mute buttons and intercoms, call-cost monitors and portable dialers. There is equipment that lets you turn your electrical appliances on and off over the phone, and screening devices that allow only those with special code numbers to get through to you. If that's not enough, there's a dashboard-mounted car phone that lets you speak into a microphone in the sun visor and hear the other person through your car's rear speakers. And if you want to always be in reach of a phone, the phone company has your number. Several hotel chains have made it a point to install phones in the bathrooms, so important executives don't miss calls. Since you don't have to be an executive to be important—or even to receive important calls—the phone company has instituted a new national marketing push to have phones installed in everybody's powder room. Picturephone service is not recommended for this purpose.

But remember, you don't have to get rid of your present phone if you're really attached to it. You may be permitted to buy it or, in some cases, to continue to rent it. It all depends upon where you live. Some states allow phone customers to purchase their phones from the phone company, either outright or on an installment plan. After the payments are made, it's yours. Of course, you'll be paying top dollar for it—perhaps 40 percent more than if you bought it elsewhere. But in some cases phone companies offer substantial discounts for a period of time after the phones go on sale, resulting in good buys on equipment.

Over the long term, buying a telephone makes sense: If you choose to buy your own equipment, meaning the end of monthly rental payments, the break-even point is typically 12 to 18 months. After that, you're saving money.

In December 1982, for example, when the C&P Telephone Company asked the Maryland Public Service Commission for permission to sell off its inventory of phones and the equipment already in customers' homes, it proposed substantial bargains for equipment bought during the first 90 days of the "sale." Here are the differences in costs:

For C&P equipment already in place:

Type of phone	Cost	
	First 90 days	After 90 days
Standard rotary	$19.95	$34.95
Princess rotary	$39.95	$59.95
Trimline rotary	$44.95	$64.95
Standard Touch-Tone	$41.95	$54.95
Princess Touch-Tone	$49.95	$69.95
Trimline Touch-Tone	$54.95	$74.95

Phone prices vary widely, even among local Bell companies. A survey by the *Wall Street Journal* found that a standard rotary phone was being sold for $18.75 by Northwestern Bell in North Dakota; in New York City, the same model was being sold for $45 by New York Bell.

Unfortunately, when the phone company offered its phones for sale in some states, most consumers refused to buy at any price. The old habit of renting was comfortable, apparently, and the prospect of buying a phone proved a bit intimidating. The phone company has done little to break customers of these old habits, since it traditionally has made more from monthly rentals than outright sales. (Why sell a phone outright for $45, when you can get $30 a year in monthly rental charges for a decade or more?) Consumer groups, meanwhile, have been after phone companies to better publicize the right of customers to buy phones, since it is to the consumer's advantage.

In those states that don't have a buying plan, you simply can't buy your present rental phone. You either must get rid of it (by returning it to the phone company) and buy a new one from the phone company or an independent equipment seller. Of course, you can continue to rent, if you have nothing better to do with your money.

The FCC is working out a nationwide scheme to cope with the millions of phone company-owned phones still out there in states that haven't yet figured out a purchase plan. So far, they haven't made much headway, mainly because they can't figure out how much your phone is worth. The problem is that the cost of one single phone is so deeply embedded in the rest of AT&T's assets—

research and development costs, telephone poles, trucks, buildings, transmitters, and all the rest—that separating it out is quite a chore. It would be like trying to establish the price of one grain of wheat lodged in a silo filled up over a 100-year period. Still, the purchase price to you of any company-owned telephone may be much higher than that of a new phone purchased elsewhere. In addition, it probably will be a plain old telephone, not a fancy new gizmo that you may really want.

Because of the divestiture agreement, as of January 1984, ownership of your rental phone changes from the local Bell company to an AT&T subsidiary known as American Bell Inc. You receive a separate rental bill from ABI, and if the rental phone goes sour you must contact one of the newly set-up ABI PhoneCenters.

Buying a phone from a local Bell telephone company is kind of confusing, due to certain complex court cases. During 1983, Bell phone companies were told they could sell off their existing inventories of telephones, but once they ran out, they couldn't sell phones to consumers until divestiture, when the local Bell companies were independent from AT&T. Either way, it is up to the local company to take care of any phones they sell. The details of their products' liability are spelled out in the warranty that comes with each phone.

Keep in mind that you probably won't be able to rent new phones from Bell telephone companies anymore. Although after divestiture they can, legally, rent phones, they most likely will decide not to. It's not only more profitable in a competitive market to sell phones to consumers rather than rent them, it's much less of a headache. You may buy phones from the local Bell telephone company (see previous paragraph for exception), from American Bell, or from any other company or store that sells phones. If you're served by an *independent* phone company you may still rent new phones, but for a monthly fee set by the company, not the state regulatory agency as before. That price will be much higher than you're paying now. Again, independents may follow the Bell companies' lead and sell, instead of rent, new phones.

That's okay. In fact, it's more than okay. You can't afford to rent a phone anymore. A simple Touch-Tone phone rents for between $2 and $4 a month. At that rate, you could buy a phone and pay for it in about 10 months. You may have already paid for one a dozen times over while renting it during the past few years. Renting a phone is a sucker's game.

Again, buying a phone from American Bell or from your local phone company—Bell or independent—will still be much higher than if you go elsewhere. Renting will be at rates set by the company, and they will be high.

The bottom line is that one way or another, one day, we'll all own our phones. Why not do it now?

There is an abundance of equipment—some good, some not so good, some illegal, and some that may not work in your home. Fortunately, there are ways to tell into which category each piece of equipment falls.

Phones, Phones, and More Phones

So, you've decided to buy a phone. Which one do you buy?

Warranties are worth considering, and assessing your real needs is obviously important. New products are being unveiled all the time, while others are awaiting FCC approval. We can't tell you exactly which brand or model to purchase, since your budget and the range of options makes it very much an individual choice. We can, however, let you know what to look for.

When it comes to regular old phones, you'll find that the plain black phone is still around, although it occupies a spot off in the back corner of the store. Designer phones of one sort or another are now the norm, with choices ranging from the Genie Phone— an Aladdin's lamp-type affair available in a number of colors and finishes, including persimmon red leather—to phones that look like footballs, ducks, and fish. (Phona-Duck actually quacks when it rings.)

These may fit in nicely with your decor (particularly if you have a duck blind in your living room), but they may not give you all the utility features you want. A lot of the designer models are nothing more than souped-up outer shells with standard insides; they're regular push-button or rotary dialing phones, except that instead of a normal mouthpiece, you talk into a beer can, a flower petal, or the back of a fish head. If you don't want or need other features, these may do just fine.

But before you grab the first designer phone that tickles your fancy, look for one that has the practical, useful options that you need. This, of course, can get tricky, since you're going to find a long list of options, and it's easy to spend a lot of money in search of the ultimate phone.

Among the options you'll find:

- hands-free operation, allowing you to use the phone without picking up the receiver;
- a hold key;
- single-button memory dialing, allowing you to store often-dialed numbers and call them without dialing the entire number;
- a last-number redial key (why redial seven or ten numbers when you can hit one button?);
- a mute button, so you don't have to cover the mouthpiece with your hand while you complain to someone in the room about the person on the other end of the line; and
- on-hook dialing, which dials for you automatically, then beeps when the connection is made or lets you hear through a speaker when the other party comes on. This frees you from sitting with the phone on your ear waiting for someone to pick up, and is particularly useful with gadgets that regularly redial a busy number at specified intervals.

Rotary dialing is still a viable option (in fact, in some isolated areas of the country Touch-Tone service is still not available), but it has its limitations. Electronic banking, for example, requires Touch-Tone service. If you don't want to actually pay your bills by phone, there may be other related services you'll find convenient. Some banks, gearing up for electronic banking, are making it possible to check your balance with a phone call. It works like this:

You call a phone number; a synthesized voice answers and asks you to punch in a code that will identify what you want to know (checking and savings balance, last deposit to checking, last deposit to savings, etc.). You are then asked for your customer reference number—perhaps a number off your automatic teller card—and then your personal identification number. When you get it all right, you get your information. All it takes is entering a code and pressing the # button on your phone.

More and more, we are seeing uses for the pound (#) and star (*) buttons on the phone, so you might want to give at least some thought to Touch-Tone service—particularly if you're considering a long distance service, or if you can avail yourself of some of the other services that require Touch-Tone.

Keep in mind, though, that Touch-Tone is a special service provided by the phone company; you can't simply go out and buy a push-button phone, plug it in, and get Touch-Tone service. But

Undertaken by an Undertaker

In 1889, Almon B. Strowger of Kansas City invented the first practical telephone switch, replacing the need for operators to connect calls.
Strowger was not a scientist or engineer but an undertaker, and he built
the "Strowger Switch" because he believed phone operators were
diverting calls for his services to competitors, who would reach the
precious bodies before he did.

you can buy push-button phones that transmit signals through
the phone lines like a dial phone, giving you the ease of push-
button without paying for it. These phones are convenient, but
because they don't transmit tones over the phone lines like Touch-
Tone (they work by generating on-off pulses), you can't use them
for special services like discount long distance dialing.

Of course, there are ways to beat even the phone company. You
can call the long distance access number on your rotary dial phone,
for example, then run to the Touch-Tone phone in another room
and dial your long distance access code. If that sounds like too
much work, there are now telephones that switch from one system
to another. This means you can call the long distance access
number, and instead of running to the other room, just flip a
switch. You can now dial in Touch-Tone mode, even though you
don't pay for Touch-Tone service.

Cutting The Cord

If the thought of stringing telephone wire from one room to
another is just a bit too overwhelming, there is at least one viable
alternative (besides calling the phone company in to do the wiring): a cordless phone.

A hand-held phone you carry with you from room to room, or
out into the garden, certainly has some obvious advantages. But
there also are some decided inconveniences and drawbacks you'll
be required to endure.

Essentially, a cordless phone is a two-part device: the stationary
base station, which plugs into a telephone jack at one end and
into an electrical outlet at the other; and the portable handset,
which has a speaker and a mouthpiece and looks like a cross between a walkie-talkie and a pocket calculator. In many models,
the electrical wiring in your home is used as an antenna to

transmit an FM signal from the base station to the handset, which is equipped with an internal antenna to receive signals and, in most cases, a telescoping antenna to transmit. Therefore, the type of wiring in your home, as well as the layout of the building, will affect the quality of your reception. Unfortunately, there is no way to know in advance if your home's insulation, for example, will affect the performance of the phone. Manufacturers do make some suggestions, such as keeping the base unit out of your basement if possible and using a long extension cord to connect the base unit. Beyond that, there may not be a lot you can do to improve performance.

Most cordless phones—at least those approved by the Federal Communications Commission—have a range of about 50 to 800 feet. There are some on the market, however, that claim to have a range of up to 25 miles. These claims may be accurate, but they are not approved by the FCC for use in the United States—yes, these phones are illegal—and you'd be better off with another model. The portable handsets, some of which are small enough to fit in your pocket, work off batteries and can be recharged in the cradle of the base station or with chargers that plug into electrical outlets. Early models did not act exactly like a standard telephone: only one person could speak at a time, and usually with a good deal of static in the background, to boot. But improvements in second- and third-generation models have meant a new standard, and one which you should be aware of: a full-duplex system, meaning that both parties can talk simultaneously, as with standard telephones.

On some models the sound is rather distorted, with a good deal of static—a marked deterioration in quality from what you're used to. The quality of sound has been likened to everything from talking in a phone booth during rush hour to talking from the bottom of a pool. In addition, the range on some models is severely limited; it's possible that a next-door neighbor who also has a cordless phone may pick up calls intended for you, or his calls will ring—and likely at 6 AM—on your phone.

But there are, as we said, distinct advantages, and the current generation of cordless phones has progressed to the point where millions of consumers have decided to take the plunge. There is no extra charge from the phone company when you buy a cordless phone (you must register it, though, just as you would register any other piece of equipment; more on that in Chapter Five), and the money you save on wiring your premises, depending on how many jacks you intend to install, could be significant. You should, however, do a little shopping around to save yourself some aggravation and disappointment.

Another major problem that has plagued users of cordless phones is the matter of privacy. The Federal Communications Commission has allotted only five channels for these devices (the industry is pushing for more), and it's possible that the unit you bought is designed to work on the same frequency as your next-door neighbor's cordless phone. Because the range of cordless phones is great enough to stretch beyond the boundaries of your property, it is possible that you may inadvertantly receive one another's calls. If that happens, your best bet is to take the phone back and trade it for one that operates on a different frequency. If all your neighbors have them, there could be some classic feuds around the hedges.

But even if you work things out with your neighbors, dial-tone thieves still may be lurking as we speak. When your unit is turned on, you hear a dial tone with the handset, just as you do with a standard phone. (Note, however, that some models are "answer-only" and don't let you originate calls.) If someone strolling through the neighborhood with a compatible cordless phone picks up the dial tone from your base unit, they can simply make a call. And guess who gets stuck with the phone bill? To guard against this, manufacturers have added features that use security codes, making rip-offs less of a problem. But if your cordless phone does not have this security feature, you could be liable for some unexplainable bills. One way to minimize the threat is to turn the phone off when you're not at home.

As with other types of phones, cordless phones have been sprouting all sorts of gizmos, everything from automatic last-number redial to built-in clocks and even an intercom function, which means you can use your phone like a walkie-talkie around the house. As with standard phones, checking warranties, which differ from manufacturer to manufacturer, is a good idea. To give you some idea of what's available (prices for cordless phones range from about $59 to $400), here's a sampling of some of the newer models and the features they offer:

- Cobra Communications offers, among others, the Cobraphone, which has a 600-foot range, two-way intercom, automatic last-number redialing and a volume switch. In addition, the unit, which comes with a one-year warranty and works on Touch-Tone or rotary lines, has a "clear-call selector," allowing for best possible voice clarity.

- Phone-Mate, better known for its answering machines, brings you the Roam Phone IQ 1140. This compact hand-held phone not only has a ten-number built-in automatic dialer, but also has a built-in digital clock and call timer, which displays the number you dialed. There's more: the Roam Phone can be used with any of the company's answering machines that allow you to screen calls, so you know who's calling before you pick up.
- A cordless phone with a mute button? Gee! No, GTE. This company has a line of cordless models, including the inch-thick Starmate. When the mute button is pressed, you can hear the person you're talking to, but they can't hear what's going on at your end. Another nice feature is a button on the base station that pages the person carrying the handset.
- And finally, the Mura Corporation has its Muraphone, which automatically hangs up at the base station if you forget to do so at the handset. The Muraphone also has a unique intercom feature: someone at the base station answers the phone, puts the call on hold and gets you on the intercom to tell you who's calling. You can take the call or pretend you're not home, or, if you wish, you can have a three-way conversation with the caller and the person at the base station.

You can't yet buy designer or novelty cordless phones, but then again, you probably wouldn't want to be seen walking around your back yard talking into your cordless Phona-Duck.

I'm Not In Right Now, But . . .

Here's what the Phone-Mate IQ 3000 answering machine, which will set you back about $400, will do:

You can record two different outgoing messages and program the machine to change the messages automatically at a specified time. (If you change your mind, you can call your machine from wherever you are and give it new instructions.) Callers can talk as long as 30 minutes—depending on the length of time you determine for messages—but if a caller hangs up without leaving a message, the machine automatically backs up. No wasted tape; no calling in to hear endless dial tones. When you do call in to

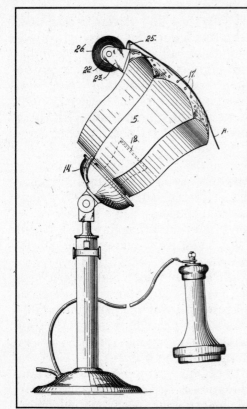

About Face

On March 26, 1912, Lincoln C. Stockton was awarded a patent for a telephone device you probably wouldn't want to share with just anyone. Stockton's "Portable Face-Mask for Telephone Use" was the latest in privacy devices, intended to substitute for those cumbersome wooden phone booths. "My invention relates to improvements in face masks for use in telephoning, the object being to prevent the sound of the voice from being heard by others in the vicinity of the party telephoning," Stockton wrote in his original patent. It also looks like it could have doubled as an ideal feed bag.

check your messages—and this isn't done with a beeper device, but with your personal security code from any Touch-Tone phone—the machine decides whether to save you money. If there are messages waiting, it will answer on the first ring. If no one called, it won't answer until the fourth ring, meaning you can hang up and save a dime—or a dollar, depending upon how long the distance. You can record a half-hour of telephone conversation with or without an electronic beep sequence, to let the other party know you're taping the call. That's not all. A digital display shows things like the number of messages recorded and the current time; when the incoming tape is full, a message so informs the caller; you decide whether to have it answer on the second, fourth, or sixth ring.

And so it goes. The simple one-cassette recording device, the intimidating machine that leaves some people unable to speak, is now loaded down with features galore. They plug into modular jacks and AC outlets, and with the right features your machine acts more like an answering service than an answering machine.

Deciding on which answering machine is best can be a maddening experience, since a number of models offer similar features—although often with slight variations. And it is the slight variations that can mean endless indecision. Certainly, you'll want to know that the machine you buy has a large enough capacity to handle expected numbers of incoming calls. But there are a few other things you may also want to look for when buying a machine:

- Call counters are an obvious option you should consider, since you don't want to waste time listening to messages that may or may not have been recorded that day. On a similar note, last-message alert lets you know when that day's messages have come to an end—a good feature if you're taping over previously recorded messages.
- The ability to scan a tape quickly is a handy feature, because you may not want to wade through a day's worth of messages in search of that one important call you've been waiting for.
- A standard feature is a silent monitor, which lets you stand by the phone and listen to the incoming message so you can decide whether or not to pick up the phone.
- Being able to set the length of both incoming messages and outgoing announcements may be of some importance. Some machines allow for variable-length announcements, which let you say exactly what you want without being locked into the manufacturer's predetermined time frame. On the other end, some machines simply offer callers 30 seconds or so to leave a message; others, however, with a "VOX" feature, allow callers to leave messages of any length. Because they are activated by the caller's voice, they shut off after the person has finished leaving a message.
- The ability to set the machine to answer on a particular ring—rather than simply the first ring—is possible with a number of models; this feature gives you the option to stop what you're doing and get to the phone before the machine clicks on.
- The method of retrieving your messages is of importance. If you're on the road a lot, a remote cordless device that lets you call your machine and listen to messages is an obvious plus. The new generation of machines don't require remote devices, but rather work with a code you punch in from any

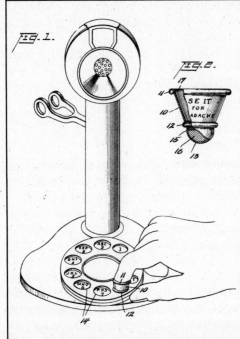

Don't Touch That Dial

Edward O. Hunter's 1929 invention was so clever that you might want to consider foresaking your push-button phone for a rotary model, just so you can put it to use. This ingenious little device was designed to save wear and tear on the index finger nail. Hunter's clever "Finger Thimble for Telephone Dials" allowed you to slip this little number on the end of your digit and dial the phone, without any discomfort whatsoever. And although he didn't mention it in his patent, you probably also could use it for sewing.

Touch-Tone phone. At present, however, these machines are expensive.

- Being able to erase those messages you've already received from a remote location also may be a useful, albeit expensive, feature.

Another option is a combination telephone and answering machine, which takes up less space than two separate units. The problem with these units is that they don't give you all the options available when you buy a separate phone and answering machine. But they do have some enhanced features. The Phonesitter, for example, which looks like a cordless phone with a cord, can be preprogrammed with outgoing messages of any length. One Phonesitter model even has remote playback from any telephone.

Of course, there are other ways of having your messages delivered that don't require answering machines. An interesting idea for small businesses is a thermal printer system, the MP 2000, distributed by Advanced Communications Inc. A unit plugs into a modular phone jack in your office and prints out messages sent directly to you by the switchboard. If you're on the phone and don't want to be buzzed, a printed message can be sent to you indicating who's on the other line. Or if you're out of the office, your messages, complete with time and date, can be sent to your printer so they'll be waiting when you get back. If you manage to lose your little printout, copies are kept at the main terminal.

Good Gizmos

There is an endless list of interesting phones and accessories on the market, and that list is expanding daily. Be aware, however, that many of these high-tech products carry high price tags. Here is a selection of some of the more imaginative gizmos we've come across, which should give you at least some idea of what's available out there.

Password, Please. If you're very choosy about who you want to talk to, PriveCode ($300), marketed by International Mobile Machines Corporation, is for you. When the unit is on, no one can get through unless they have a code number—and even then you'll know who's on the other end of the line. Callers are greeted by a synthesized female voice asking for a previously assigned three-digit code number. The caller must then punch in the specific code you've assigned. If a valid code number isn't entered after three tries, the machine automatically hangs up. If a valid code number is entered, it is displayed on an LED screen, letting you know in advance who is trying to reach you.

If It's So Smart, Why Ain't It Rich? An enhanced version of PriveCode is Smartguard, a phone from Technicom International that operates as a normal telephone, but also can be used as a screening device. When someone calls, they need a pre-arranged dialing code or your phone won't even ring. You can tell who's calling simply by looking at the display window in the phone. In addition to the screening function, Smartguard has hands-free operation via a built-in speakerphone, emergency number dialing, a hold key, single-button memory dialing, last-number redial, a call timer and alarm, calendar/date display, a directory tray, a mute button, on-hook dialing, and a timed flash key. In addition, the phone records access codes for later display so you can tell who called when you weren't at home.

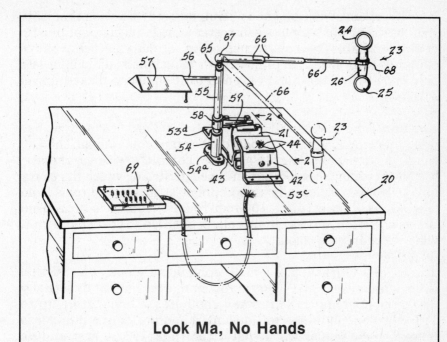

Look Ma, No Hands

If you can't always get up to dial the phone, Frank G. Holmes just may have your number. In 1953, the Philadelphia inventor patented his "Remote Control Electronic Telephone Dialing Means." This ingenious precursor of push-button dialing allows you to forego the old rotary dial and still complete your call. Then you swing the metal arm your way and you're ready for hands-free talking. Rube Goldberg probably would have appreciated it.

And You Can Even Blast The Neighbors With Loud Music When You're On Vacation. For about $100, Radio Shack will let you control up to eight 120-volt appliances via the phone. The Plug 'n Power Telephone Remote Control Center plugs into any standard telephone jack and AC outlet. If you want to start the microwave before you get home from work, or turn the lights on and off when you're gone for a few days, it's as easy as making a call and pressing a few buttons. Another good idea from Radio Shack, particularly for small businesses, is the DuOFONE TAD-100 announce-only phone answer. For about $50, you can attach a machine to your phone that will play a recorded announcement but won't take messages.

Bug Repellent. Worried about being bugged? For less than $50, Phone Guard will let you sleep better at night. This clear plastic device, available from many mail-order catalogs featuring phone equipment, screws on in place of your mouthpiece; a red light lets you know when the line is tapped or if someone picked up an extension.

You Can Take It With You—But Only 100 Feet. Technidyne has done for telephones what Sony did for portable radios. The Go-Fone—a three-ounce cordless gizmo, complete with earphone—is a close cousin of the Walkman. The unit ($150), which fits easily in your pocket, is actually a microphone that relays signals from the base station within a 100-foot radius. Dialing is done from the base station and incoming calls are routed to the remote unit, which recharges overnight.

The Devil's Workshop. Zoom Telephonic's Demon Dialer ($199) is one appliance that can keep you from ever having to actually dial a phone number. This small computer lets you store up to 176 telephone numbers for automatic dialing. If the number is busy, Demon Dialer will redial it ten times in the first minute and every two minutes for the next two hours. (If you want it to, it will keep dialing every ten minutes for up to ten hours.) And while the computer is trying to get through, it will continue to monitor for incoming calls. When your call is finally placed, Demon Dialer will signal you, meaning you can go about your business while it does the work.

But It Won't Mix A Martini. For business-minded folks, TIE/Technicom offers the Execufone (about $230), which does everything but calculate your golf handicap. This telephone/alarm clock/calculator/speakerphone has such features as on-hook dialing, a built-in directory, last-number-called redialing, and a toll timer to clock the length of calls.

Thanks For The Memory. If access to data banks is of interest, but you don't want a full-blown home computer, Scanset, available from the Products That Think catalog, will fill the bill. This $650 terminal, complete with keyboard, automatically places calls to humans or data banks. It even has internal memory for storage of information you get from data banks and can be attached to a printer to give you a copy of everything on the screen.

It's O.K., I Had To Get Up To Answer The Phone. In the let's-save-space category, Teleconcepts offers the Gabbiclock ($70), the ideal night-table item. This one-piece telephone and digital alarm clock includes everything from snooze alarm to a mute button and last-number redialing. No, you can't place a wake-up call to yourself.

Remind Me To Fire The Answering Service. If "call forwarding" is not yet available in your area, you're not totally out of luck. A number of manufacturers offer call diverters that essentially accomplish the same thing. Peter W. Holm International manufactures two such call diverters: the PWH 2001 is a standard telephone with a feature that routes your calls to a specified number; and the PWH 3001 allows you to call the diverter and change the phone number to which calls should be transferred.

Bells, Beeps, And Whistles. In addition to a long list of designer telephones, Radio Shack is a good place to shop for installation hardware such as jacks, cords, adapters, and the like. In the I-wonder-where-I-can-get-it category, Radio Shack has the following items that may be of interest: the Tele-Recorder 150 hooks into your phone and tape recorder, starts recording when the receiver is lifted off the hook, and stops recording when you hang up; the Telephone Recording Pickup Coil is a suction cup—less than $2—that fastens instantly to your phone to record calls; Time-A-Phone, about the size of a quarter (and less than $10), fits inside your receiver and automatically beeps every three minutes to remind you that the meter is running; the Snap-On Amplifier, made for persons with hearing difficulties, amplifies incoming calls; Glayzit Telephone Refinisher is an aerosol spray that keeps your phone shining; and the Electronic Bell Tweeter/Flasher not only replaces the loud bell with a soft "tweet," but also flashes when there is an incoming call.

"Dad, Can I Have The Keys To The Phone?" If you're concerned about people running up your phone bill without your knowledge, Toll Guard ($40 for dial phones, $60 for Touch-Tone) is the answer. The system is hooked up to the phone, and can be disconnected with a special key. If the key isn't turned, it's impossible to have any call go through that's more than seven digits or that starts with zero or one. In other words, no long distance calls can be made without you knowing about it.

No-Bell Prize. Zoom Telephonics, the folks who gave you the Demon Dialer, also give you a way of getting a little peace and quiet. The Silencer Cord (around $9) plugs into modular phones and, with a flip of the switch, guarantees that you won't hear the phone ring. (The caller hears a ring, but you don't hear anything.) If you don't want another wire in the way, Zoom's Universal Silencer does the same thing as The Silencer Cord, but it fits right on the side of the phone; push the button and the bell won't ring.

Leaving The Single Life. One problem with some of the new single-line gizmos is that you can't simply bring them to your office and plug them into your multi-line system. But help is on the way. The Multi-Line Controller (about $50) lets you plug any of these accessories—including answering machines and automatic dialers—directly into your office system. With this device, which attaches with a screwdriver in about two minutes, you can dedicate the use of any line to any accessory.

The Mayday Machine. The Mura Corporation is marketing a phone that should help you feel a bit more secure. The Sage-1 ($250) is an enhanced telephone with such features as a 31-number memory dialer and last-number redial. But it also has voice capabilities that let it automatically dial any of four phone numbers and give an emergency message, simply by hitting a button on the phone or from a remote emergency pager about the size of a cigarette pack. If you worry about an elderly or sick relative, for example, the Sage will give them—and you—the comfort of knowing they can always get a message though (the message says help is needed at the following phone number). Similarly, if a burglar has entered your home, it's easy enough to call the police without having to dial the phone.

Keep Your Hands To Yourself. If you want to take dictation over the phone, or need both hands free for any other reason while talking, Plantronics/Santa Cruz has your number. The StarSet Star-Mate headset plugs right into modular telephones and slips onto your ear for easy talking and listening—it's the same kind of contraption that professional operators and receptionists use. A similar piece of equipment is manufactured by ACS Communications; its TeleTret (about $125) ultralight headset, which has a nice, cushiony foam earpiece, connects right to your phone without any special adapters.

Just Listen for the Beep

When can you legally tape a conversation off the phone? It's certainly easy enough to do; it can be accomplished with the use of a two-dollar suction cup device, as well as with most models of answering machines. The Federal Communications Commission requires phone companies to include information in their tariffs outlining what is acceptable, and enforcement is left to each local phone company.

State laws differ, but the rule of thumb is that a short beep heard every 15 seconds indicates that the person on the other end is recording the conversation. In some states, mutual consent can substitute for the beep tone; you need only ask permission of the other party, and the taping is perfectly legal. Of course, the technology has made it virtually impossible in some cases to detect whether someone is taping (it's easy enough to have a tape recorder going in a room with your speakerphone, and even the most sophisticated devices won't be able to tell the difference), but the penalties for taping your own conversations are minimal. If you are caught, which is difficult in itself, the penalty may—and the word "may" deserves some emphasis—be suspension of phone service.

Third-party wiretapping—taping a conversation of which you are not a part—is another story. This is an area in which the federal government takes a great interest. Quite simply, it's a crime under federal and state laws to intercept calls unless you happen to be a party to the conversation or unless you first obtained the consent of one of the parties taking part in the call. Law enforcement officials can listen in on your conversations after having secured the proper court order, but you have to be a hot number to warrant that sort of attention. If you do decide to listen in on your suspected-of-cheating spouse (and the equipment to do it with is not too difficult to come by), be forewarned that for your troubles, you could get five years behind bars and a $10,000 fine.

The Light Fantastic. For the executive who has everything, there's Controlonics Corporation's Litephone. In many cases, conference calling is less than desirable because the sound is a bit fuzzy. But Litephone offers a nice option. Instead of huddling around a speaker, this compact phone sits on your table or desk and beams incoming voices to a wall-mounted speaker via infrared light. The sound is crisp and clear, unlike many other speakerphone devices, which make it sound like you're calling from a phone booth in Times Square. The speaker volume is controlled by the hand-held unit, which sits there unobtrusively like a pocket calculator. Price: a whopping $600.

The Little Black (Electronic) Book. Dictograph Corporation has some interesting features on its automatic dialer, Phone Controller ($100). It's all done with on-hook dialing, and if you get a busy signal you can hit a button for automatic redialing, or you can hit another button and the dialer will keep redialing once a minute for 14 minutes. The device stores 30 pre-programmed numbers, which you may not want others to see inadvertantly. To make sure that doesn't happen, it has a privacy mode, and no one can get access to the numbers without your special code.

Reach Out And Touch Someone. There are a number of gadgets that screw onto the mouthpiece of your phone, allowing Touch-Tone dialing on a rotary model. One of the most useful is the Soft Touch Auto Dialer (about $120), which lets you store up to 40 frequently called numbers—including those never-ending Sprint and MCI access numbers. This is better than taking your address book along when you travel: it's two-and-a-half ounces and screws on in a matter of seconds. A similar gizmo is the PortaTouch, a three-ounce automatic phone dialer that dials ten 16-digit numbers from memory. PortaTouch (about $90) doesn't actually screw onto the phone; instead, you simply hold it over the mouthpiece—on either Touch-Tone or rotary dial phones—and it does the rest. It works with Sprint, MCI, or bank-by-phone numbers. Both are available from telephone mail-order catalogs.

Hold On, I'm Coming. One new idea lets you, in effect, have two lines while paying for just one. Hold-A-Phone II (about $50), manufactured by Tone Commander Systems, and Viking Electronics' Model 2L-H hold adapter both give two-line service to any telephone. These units, which are easily installed, give you a hold function and offer visual (flashing light) ringing and hold indication.

No Change Needed. The British have a couple of intriguing telephone ideas. Cotswold House sells a six-foot, full-color wallpaper backdrop—complete with fittings—that looks like a phone booth has been moved into your home. The actual phone—which you must supply—rests on a shelf "inside" the booth, which sells for about $50.

GETTING WIRED

*O*wning your own phone is as easy as this: You unplug your current equipment, bring it back to the phone company; they'll credit you on your next bill. You can buy a new model from the manufacturer of your choice, plug it in, and register the new phone with the phone company.

Because the telephone environment has changed so dramatically, chances are you may not be familiar with all the equipment and services now available, nor will you have the advice of friends who can make recommendations. Our advice, then, is to do a little exploring before you actually buy. A visit to a store that sells phones will give you an idea of all your options and help you determine whether descriptions of products advertised in periodicals and mail-order catalogs are accurate. Finding a store that sells phones is as easy as looking—where else?—in the Yellow Pages of your local directory under Telephones.

Once you have decided on the type of phone you want, there are a number of important considerations—the first of which is whether it will actually work in your home. One important factor is the Ringer Equivalence Number (REN), which is found on the registration label on the bottom of every piece of phone equipment. The key here is that the telephone company supplies each home with a limited amount of power to make your phones ring—usually enough to keep five phones humming (5 REN), although the number varies. A standard phone may use 1 REN, meaning you could connect five of them in your home and expect everything to work just fine. But if you already have two 2-REN

Court-Authorized Wiretaps Installed, 1979

New Jersey	144	Virginia	5
New York	118	District of Columbia	3
Florida	63	Nevada	2
Maryland	23	Hawaii	2
Massachusetts	22	Rhode Island	2
Nebraska	21	Delaware	2
Connecticut	15	New Mexico	1
Arizona	12	Oregon	1
Georgia	10		

phones (for a total of 4 REN) hooked up, plugging in a third 2-REN phone (for a total of 6 REN) would give you problems. A lot of the newer models use less than 1 REN, but you shouldn't take chances. Before actually buying a phone, call the local phone company business office to find out your maximum REN, then check the REN on each phone connected in your home and the REN of the equipment you're considering buying. If the numbers don't add up, you'll have to rethink your purchase (or consider disconnecting one or more phones you already have).

Another important subject is warranties. When the man with the equipment belt left the big black Western Electric phone in your home, you didn't have to worry about repairs. Renting a phone from Ma Bell meant a monthly service charge built into your basic phone bill, but it also meant the security of not having to worry about breakdowns. If the equipment went on the fritz, it was fixed or replaced for free.

However, when you buy your own equipment, you may have lost the rental charge, but you've gained all responsibilities for repairs. If the phone breaks, you have to take it in for service. If it's the only phone in your home, you may be in a bind, since it could take a week or two to fix. With that in mind, you ought to pay close attention to warranties when buying telephones and equipment.

Manufacturers' warranties differ considerably. Some will give you a loaner phone while yours is being fixed, others won't. Some warranties may last only 90 days, others for a year or longer. Some phones will be repaired and returned quickly, while others could take weeks to return. Retailers also have different warranties, and you'd be wise to compare before you buy. If you have only one phone in your home, warranties and repair facilities should

How Wiretapping Works

Listening to phone calls isn't very difficult to do, although it is clearly illegal. The quickest method wiretappers use is simply to cut into someone's phone line, preferably where the owner can't detect it (near the garage or behind the pole, for example) and wire in their own headset. Then they remove the mouthpiece, so the person being tapped can't detect the wiretapper's breathing or other noise. If a wiretapper can't stick around, he'll use a high-impedance coupling transformer and feed the wire into a tape recorder. To save tape, most tappers use the type of recorder that records automatically when it hears a voice.

Another procedure is to find the right "pair." That's telephone-tapping talk for the two wires that go into your house and that of others in your building or apartment. The boxes that contain pair terminals are called terminal boxes and can usually be found in basements of apartments or office buildings, or occasionally on the outside wall of a building.

A wiretapper typically will have an accomplice call the number being tapped. That puts about 90 volts on the line. The tapper takes two fingers and runs them down the rows of terminals. When he hits the right phone pair, he feels a jolt. Once he's found it, he's got the right phone; a listening device is then attached.

For those who prefer the wireless approach, a "bug" placed in a phone will transmit conversations over short distances. Bugs come in all sizes and shapes. A cheap type sometimes goes by the name of "Wireless Microphone." Let's face it; it's a bug. Anyone can buy them at Radio Shack or even some toy stores for less than $15. Its range is limited, usually 500 to 1,000 feet, but it will fit inside a phone and send a clear signal to an FM radio. Or better yet, it is possible to connect the wireless mike through a high-impedance transformer connected to the phone line, and no one has to enter the tapee's house.

A wiretapper also can buy bugs that look like telephone mouthpieces. They're inserted by unscrewing the mouthpiece and replacing it with a souped-up version. It goes without saying that one needs to use the right color plastic.

be of particular importance. Waiting two weeks to fix your only phone obviously will leave you in a bit of a jam. Fortunately, phones rarely break unless abused, and with any luck—unless you happen to get a lemon—you probably won't be bothered too much with repair problems.

But beware: Some cheap, easily broken phone models are coming onto the market. Even Western Electric, American Bell's main equipment supplier, is reportedly building phones to last only five years instead of twenty years, as had been their previous standard.

You Have The Right To Remain Silent ...

Another important question that you'll have to deal with is whether the equipment you're planning to buy—or the equipment you've already bought—is legal. There is no one answer universally applicable, but the Federal Communications Commission has some easy-to-follow guidelines that should make life easier.

The crucial consideration when buying equipment is whether it has been approved by the FCC. This certification has more to do with usable equipment than mere sanctions by Uncle Sam: if it does not meet government specifications, it may not work. And beyond that, if it's the wrong equipment, it may affect all other phones in your home or office. Above all, if a piece of equipment is not FCC approved, it's simply illegal to connect it to the phone lines.

To connect registered phones and other equipment, you need only call the phone company and tell them the make, model, FCC registration number, and Ringer Equivalence Number. All of this information is found on a label under the phone. The label might look something like this:

COMPLIES WITH PART 68 FCC RULES
FCC Reg. #ASA9PD-69753-TE-T
Ringer Equiv. 1.0B
GRANTEE: STANWOOD ELECTRONICS
SINGLE LINE TONE USOC RJ11C

If there is no label with this sort of information, the device is not FCC registered. But all is not lost. To ensure at least some standards of quality, the FCC maintains a list of businesses qualified to do telephone repairs. FCC-authorized refurbishers can make the necessary modifications to bring your phone into com-

---

We've Got Your Number—I

"You won't get me to stay on the line while you trace the call, you dirty copper. I ain't stupid." *Click.*

"Did you trace the call, Smitty?"

"Not enough time, Lieutenant."

And so it went in the days of grade-B detective movies and old-style telephone switches, when it took 20 minutes or more to trace a call to the phone from which it originated. Now, with almost half of all telephone central offices equipped with the latest electronic switches, tracing a call in most major cities may take less than a minute. Already, telephone operators in certain areas can see the number of the calling party on a lighted display when handling collect or person-to-person call requests. That nifty feature, however, won't be in homes for many years.

---

pliance with the proper standards. Once that's done, they will attach an FCC registration label. Others may be able to repair your equipment, but they won't be able to certify it legally as being FCC-acceptable, so be choosy about whom you deal with.

In addition, there are phones that lack FCC registration but which are still legal. Such equipment has to be already installed by your phone company and must appear on the FCC "Grandfathered Equipment List." If legally installed before July 1, 1979—with the knowledge of the phone company—the equipment can remain in use for as long as you pay your phone bills. If you move, you can take a purchased "grandfathered" phone with you and, after notifying the local telephone company, connect it to your system.

Keep in mind that FCC approval of a telephone does not necessarily imply quality. It merely signifies that the equipment meets the Commission's technical standards; the authorization does not carry with it a guarantee of any sort.

These grandfathering provisions apply to other devices, as well. On July 1, 1979, the FCC published a list of grandfathered devices, Volume I of which covers ancillary devices and Volume V of which covers telephones. There is no need, however, to plunk down five dollars for a long list of authorized numbers. If a local FCC office can't give you an answer about your equipment, try the FCC in Washington (202-632-6440); someone there should be able to give you the lowdown.

And what happens, you ask, if you use a phone that is neither grandfathered equipment nor FCC-authorized? The telephone company may never find out, but then again, it may. If you are discovered, chances are you won't go to jail, nor will your Dial-A-Joke privileges be revoked. You will, however, be asked to comply with the rules or face suspension—perhaps even termination—of phone service. It is possible for the phone company to check on your equipment from its central office by using special circuit-testing devices, and they do periodic sweeps. Although the phone never actually rings in your home, the sleuths at the phone company can get a reading on what's cooking on the other end. If their records show that you're supposed to have only one phone in your home, they'll know if more are connected.

The phone company's tariffs, filed with local public utility commissions, outline exactly what is expected of consumers, what rates can be set, and other minutiae of operations. Tariffs, which differ from one jurisdiction to another, ordinarily are available for inspection at phone company headquarters. They are not documents you'd likely care to kill an afternoon reading, however.

If you're part of a party line, you also have to pay particular attention to new equipment you're considering hooking up. Answering machines connected to party lines, for example, will not only answer your calls, but most likely your neighbors' as well. This naturally can leave your neighbors—not to mention their relatives, who ended up calling long distance just to talk with your answering machine—a bit unhappy. To ensure against such problems, the FCC decided that only your phone company can provide equipment for direct connection to a party line. So, before running out for the latest and greatest in high-tech equipment, better check first with the phone company to see if installation of that equipment is feasible.

Mother, Please, I'd Rather Do It Myself

If your home or office is equipped with the standard "modular" outlets, you really need to do nothing more than plug the phone in. It's as easy as pushing the clear plastic plug directly into the jack until it clicks into place. Removing the plug is done by pinching the plug's small plastic lever and pulling it from the jack.

If you do not have modular outlets, there are simple modifications that will make your existing outlets compatible with your new equipment. Many homes, for example, are equipped with four-hole jacks, into which a four-prong plug fits. To convert these outlets for use with modular plugs, you need only buy an adapter and plug it in (see illustration). Similarly, to adapt a four-prong telephone plug for use with a modular jack, you only need a simple adapter that plugs into the four-pronged plug. Another adapter that may be of use is the T-adapter (more on that later), which has an extra slot, enabling you to add an automatic dialer or an answering machine to your present system without having additional outlets installed. These adapters are standard equipment and available at most stores that sell phones and accessories.

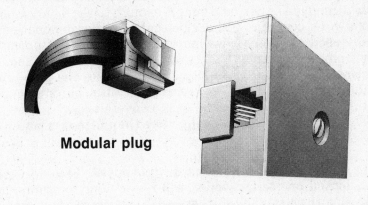

Modular plug

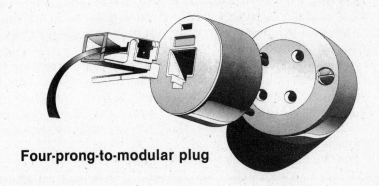

Four-prong-to-modular plug

The other type of jack you may have in your home, particularly if you haven't had new equipment installed in the last 10 years, is the hard-wire jack. These are easy to spot: the phone cord goes directly into a permanent outlet, either in the wall or in an outlet with a cover that protrudes slightly from the wall. In both cases, the phone is anchored permanently; it can't be moved from one room to another.

Converting hard-wire outlets for use with modular equipment is a bit harder, but nothing that someone capable of assembling knock-down furniture can't do with a little patience. It basically involves attaching color-coded wires to screws or connectors. You need only a screwdriver to complete the job.

Modular jacks are a convenience, since you can take a phone from one room to the next and simply pop the plug into the outlet. Converting any hard-wired connections to modular is probably a good idea, then, and simple enough to cause you minimum anxiety. Of course, if you decide that a cordless phone is all you really need at home—allowing you to take the equipment with you from room to room—you probably can just forget about converting your outdated outlets. If you foresee the possibility of adding new accessories—answering machines, automatic dialers, and the like—plan to do the easy conversions.

The whole job shouldn't take more than fifteen minutes. Here are step-by-step instructions:

1. Remove the cover of a hard-wired outlet. To do this, simply loosen one screw, which will reveal four terminal screws.
2. Before you go any further—with this procedure or any other involving wiring—it's a good idea to reduce the risk of electrical shock. The easiest way to cut down on current without cutting off phone service completely is to simply take the receiver off the hook.
3. You should now see four terminal screws. The screws (or the plastic next to each screw) are coded, leaving little doubt which wire connects to which screw: R (red), Y (yellow), B (black), and G (green). Remove the four existing wires from the screws; don't remove the screws, just loosen them enough to remove the wires.
4. Place the modular jack you're installing close enough to the terminal to connect the four color-coded wires to the terminal screws—red to the terminal marked "R," yellow to "Y," etc.
5. Put the new jack cover on the terminal, and tighten the screw.

Congratulations: You can now plug in your modular phone.

Some jacks are even easier to install: instead of screwing the wires on, you simply snap four color-coded connector buttons onto the screws. The new cover is then screwed on, the entire process taking just a couple of minutes.

Find a Friend at the Phone Company

When connecting your new phones, or putting in new jacks, the best way to check your work is have a friend call you. However, phone companies also maintain special numbers that ring your phone when dialed from your phone. Usually, it's a special three-digit number plus the last four digits of your phone number. A friendly phone company employee may let you in on the secret.

With hard-wire outlets that fit flush with the wall, the process is essentially the same: the end result is that the color-coded wires attach to the proper terminal screws. If you have any problems, most phone stores that sell this hardware can show you exactly how the installation should be done. Of course, before you decide to actually add the new jacks, you might want to check with the telephone company to see if they'll do it for free. In some states, in fact, they're required to make the changes without charge.

Not every state allows telephone customers to install their own jacks. New York State was the first to give consumers the right to install, rearrange, or repair jacks, and about two-thirds of the states have followed suit (see box). The FCC has been looking into the possibility of establishing nationwide standards and procedures whereby consumers could install their own jacks and wiring without state permission. A check with your phone company will tell you whether it is now legal in your area.

Apartment dwellers may have different circumstances, and generally less flexibility. It is within a landlord's legal rights to refuse a tenant's request to add additional jacks in his apartment. This may be spelled out in your lease, so check the document carefully. Some apartments have switchboard systems, which provide the luxury of an answering service. But the phone lines with set-ups of this sort may preclude the installation of that much-wanted Pac-Man phone, so here too, check first with the landlord and/or the phone company.

If it's not legal in your area for you to install jacks, and the phone company does it, you can still save money by planning ahead. Figure out in advance where you want each jack, since you will be charged for additional installation visits each time the phone technician has to come back.

As with phones, if you install the jack yourself, you're responsible if it goes sour. If the phone company does the installation,

States That Allow Customer Wiring

Not every state allows telephone customers to do their own inside wiring, but most are considering the possibility. Here are the states—for Bell-served areas—that allow one- and two-line residential wiring or have such programs in the planning or pending stages. In addition, provisions have been made in some non-Bell-served areas by General Telephone and other independents for customers to do inside wiring. Check with the phone company or the state public utility commission for details about such programs in your area.

Alabama	Nebraska
Arizona	Nevada
Arkansas	New Hampshire
California	New Jersey
Connecticut	New Mexico
Colorado	New York
Delaware	North Carolina
District of Columbia	North Dakota
Florida	Ohio
Georgia	Oklahoma
Idaho	Oregon
Illinois	Pennsylvania
Indiana	Rhode Island
Iowa	South Carolina
Kansas	South Dakota
Kentucky	Tennessee
Louisiana	Texas
Massachusetts	Utah
Maine	Vermont
Maryland	Virginia
Michigan	Washington
Minnesota	West Virginia
Mississippi	Wisconsin
Missouri	Wyoming
Montana	

it's their headache. However, jacks break down even less often than phones, so if your initial installation is sound, it should stay that way.

There are a number of ways to connect additional phones, the easiest being the T-adapter (see illustration). You can easily run an extension wire from this adapter, which converts a modular jack into a receptacle for two plugs. Simply plug the extension wire into one end of the jack, then staple the wire along the baseboard as if you were laying stereo speaker wire. The extension wire can then connect to a back-to-back modular jack, which is a receptacle for two modular base cords. The telephone is plugged into the other side of this small jack, and the phone is ready to use.

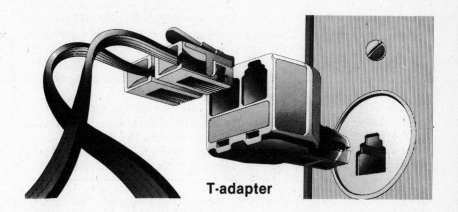

T-adapter

Additional jacks can be installed by running color-coded, four-conductor copper wire from one room to another. A 50-foot roll of wire should cost you about $4 and a modular jack assembly costs about $6. If you're thinking of installing several jacks, it may be useful to use a wire junction—a central connecting point for a number of wires running to modular jacks. You can, for example, connect three outlets for phone extensions to a single wire junction and run a fourth set of wires to another junction, where additional jacks can be connected. This saves you the problem of separate jack installations in every room. Keep in mind, however, that just because you have jacks all over the place doesn't mean you can connect phones to all of them. Consider that your Ringer Equivalence Number limit is probably 5 REN.

Installing new jacks will require some tools, since you'll need to cut and strip wires, perhaps drill holes for screws, or even cut a hole in the wall. If you're planning on doing a lot of wiring, check first to see if there are any applicable local building codes that you should know about. Check also to see if there is a way to disconnect existing wiring to avoid possible shocks. It's also a good idea to use a screwdriver with an insulated handle and to keep your bare hands off screw terminals. But don't worry: Virtually all home telephone wiring is low voltage; if you ever received a shock, it would merely tingle; if the phone rings while you're

We've Got Your Number—II

Although many people think of legal wiretaps as the most common way for the phone company to check your calling activity, there are others. Under court order, the phone company may attach a "Pen Register" to your phone wires at the central office. The device gives a printout of all calls, local and long distance, going out of your phone including time of day, duration of call, and, of course, the recipient's number. It's used mostly by law enforcement agencies to check who you are calling in hopes that the other party will shed some light on your alleged wrongdoing.

Law enforcement agencies often prefer the Pen Register to an out-and-out wiretap. It takes less work, less manpower (the Pen Register is automatic; the gumshoes just come by the phone company and pick up the printout), and less hassle to obtain a court order for its installation, because it's less of an invasion of privacy than a wiretap.

working, you could receive an uncomfortable jolt, but nothing that will cause serious harm.

If it all goes smoothly, you can save yourself some money and have phone jacks wherever you want them. If it doesn't go smoothly, you may find yourself with wires strewn around the living room and a house full of phones that don't work. The best guide, we guess, is to take on a job you feel comfortable with. If plugging in a toaster is a major production, better leave the wiring to the phone company or to a friend who has the tools and experience to do the job right.

Talking Back to the Phone Company

The bottom line with the new telephone environment—at least in terms of consumer rights—is that many of the old rules still apply: If you want to complain about your bill, you still complain to your local phone company; if you want to complain about the phone company, the public utility commission is the place to go; if long distance service has you puzzled, the FCC still keeps an eye on interstate calling. If you're uncertain about where to turn, the best method is to work from the bottom up. If you're bothered by "junk" calls, for example, with machines calling you at dinnertime with a sales pitch of some sort, start with your local phone company and, if you don't get satisfaction, work your way up the ladder. If all else fails, write your congressional representatives; they have "caseworkers" on hand to help cut through red tape. Telecommunications issues have been hot items on Capitol Hill the last few years and most members of Congress have been keeping up with the goings-on in this area.

If you want to complain about the rates you pay for phone service, the phone company probably isn't the place to go. The phone company files for rate increases with the state public utility commission,which decides whether to grant these requests after hearings and deliberations. If you're the type who wants to get involved in such issues, the public utility commission is the place to take your grievances. If you don't nip a rate increase in the bud there, don't be surprised to receive a notice like this in the mail at periodic intervals:

NOTICE OF RATE CHANGE

On November 13, 1982, new rates for telephone equipment, service and message units became effective as authorized by the District of Columbia Public Service Commission. The average of this increase for residential customers is less than 3 percent. Individual customers may see charges which differ from this average due to the particular services used.

These rates are the result of the Commission's final decision on C&P Telephone's application to increase telephone rates filed November 12, 1981. That decision authorized an adjustment in local telephone rates on August 14, 1982, with final rates to become effective on November 13, 1982.

Examples of the rates are shown on the back of this notice. Rates for long-distance calls are not affected by these changes.

If you would like a detailed explanation or the changes, please dial the telephone number of the top right portion of your bill. A service representative will be pleased to assist you.

Challenging the phone company before a state utility commission is a time-consuming, complicated process, and one that you wouldn't want to do without a lot of help. Specifically, this means that there is strength in numbers, and it takes a good coalition of people to withstand the entire process.

You can't challenge everything, though. For example, the FCC allows local phone companies to change their facilities or equipment when those changes are reasonably required in the operation of their business. If those changes are expected to cause your equipment to go on the fritz, the phone company is required to notify you in writing by mail. (Don't expect ever to see a notice of this sort if you live in a reasonably heavily populated area.) This, of course, conceivably could cause you some inconvenience. But by all means don't scrap your equipment. It is likely that an FCC-authorized refurbisher or the manufacturer can make the necessary changes to keep your phone working. However, you probably shouldn't worry about it. It rarely happens except in small towns and rural areas.

If you still don't get satisfaction, or if you're just plain confused about whether everything about your phone service is kosher, consumer groups may be your best bet. That's even more important since the break-up of AT&T. Whereas telephones were for a long time little more than the taken-for-granted, ubiquitous tools of that ever-criticized Ma Bell, it's now going to be possible for Ma to point the finger of blame in a number of directions: your local phone company (no longer part of AT&T), the manufacturer of your phone equipment, etc. Getting problems resolved may require wading through various bureaucracies of one sort or another, and it's a task that could take you more time than it's worth.

If you are simply contesting a phone bill, you can do that yourself. Here are some key points to keep in mind:

- When dealing directly with the phone company, the first thing to remember is that the phone company—and that includes your discount long distance company as well as the local phone company—is not always right. Mysterious calls to unknown numbers can turn up on your phone bill, and there is no reason to pay them blindly. A call to your local phone company service representative often will resolve the problem.
- If you don't get satisfaction from the service representative, ask for the supervisor. If that doesn't do the trick, move up a notch to the manager. (Always remember to get the names of those you speak with, and keep track of the date and time of your conversation. And if you write to the phone company on a disputed matter, make sure to keep copies of your correspondence.) The phone company actually is quite good about deleting contested calls from your bill, although the whys and wherefores of its decision-making process appear to be extremely arbitrary, to say the least.

Is Anybody Out There Listening?

Simply put, if you think your phone is being tapped, contact the phone company. If it's a legal, albeit rare, court-ordered tap, the phone company is in on it, and they won't help you. In fact, they won't even verify it's on the line. But if it isn't legal, they may be as eager as you to get rid of it. But then again, if it's the Central Intelligence Agency, Internal Revenue Service, National Security Agency, or Federal Bureau of Investigation, phone companies have been known to look the other way.

So, you're really on your own no matter who is doing the bugging.

If an amateur has you bugged, he probably is tapping your line near your home. Follow your wires as far as you can see. Check the small box coming into your house. (It's called the surge protector.) Then, check the terminal box for signs of wires that look like they don't belong. Next, physically search the phone, take it apart and look inside. Unscrew the mouthpiece and the earphone.

If it looks like it might be a professional job, you can call in a professional de-bugger. He'll know how to use a "sweeper," a device that detects transmitters. And, he'll have connections in the phone company to help him find the so-called "B" box, or "bridging head," sometimes known as an "appearance" or "multiple." These large junction boxes house many terminal connections from many phones in the neighborhood, and they can be several blocks from your phone. That's where legal taps and those from other professionals usually take place. Unless you have a wiring diagram of your neighborhood phone network, it's difficult to find the box that feeds your line.

Once your line is debugged, the bugger could return. So, to take the worry out of phoning, use a bugging detector that you can attach directly to your phone line. It will signal if there is a tap.

You also may consider a scrambler-phone. The best ones take your voice, turn it into electronic pulses, scramble the pulses up according to a designated scheme, and send them out across the phone lines. On the other end, the de-scrambler, which knows the designated scheme, takes the signal and puts it back together in the right order to form speech. Of course, you'll have to provide a de-scrambler to everyone with whom you may have sensitive conversations. These gizmos are widely sold to businesses and governments to scramble their everyday conversations. They also work on Telex and TWX. They'll do wonders for your ego because they have replaced paper shredders as the new status symbol of the information age.

- If it's an international bill that's in question, start with the same procedure. Keep in mind, though, that the FCC, which leaves local telephone matters to state utility commissions (for the most part), does have a specific interest in international telephony. If you feel you're being treated unfairly with a disputed international call, you should take your case to the FCC by writing the closest regional office or the main headquarters in Washington, D.C.

- Some discount long-distance services have a similar disputed-call policy: Just inform them of the contested calls and withhold payment for the amount you're disputing. It's possible that the company's computers billed someone else's calls to your number; it's also possible that someone managed to get your personal code, in which case you'd be wise to contact the company immediately and arrange for a new code. Often, coast-to-coast calls made using these services have a bad echo, making it necessary to redial. Service representatives suggest you keep track of these and subtract them from your bill with an explanation. Of course, don't just withhold partial payment without first talking to someone from the company and explaining the circumstances.
- If all else fails, there is always court. It is possible to resolve some cases in small claims court—although some courts will want to know that you've been through the proper regulatory channels before seeking judicial help. It probably isn't worth it to tie yourself up in small claims court over an insignificant amount of money, but if a few hundred dollars is at stake, that may be your logical, last recourse.

WHAT THE (BEEP) IS GOING ON?

In the spring of 1950, medical history was made. While playing golf, a New York doctor became the first person ever to be alerted by a pocket pager. He was taken away from his game by an emergency call.

Since then, hundreds of thousands of times every day, doctors, salespeople, technicians, police detectives, and others on the go are "beeped" while away from their offices.

Millions of Americans carry pocket pagers, also called "beepers." Even upper-crust parents in Beverly Hills regularly beep their pager-toting children to come home for dinner. Some folks use pagers as alarm clocks; they ask a friend or hire a telephone service to call their beeper at the same time every day; no matter where they fall asleep they are never late for work. Pagers thin enough to fit in the back pocket of designer jeans have become the new status symbol. One company even sells empty pager cases for those who want others to think they're important enough to be paged.

Simply put, pagers are extremely sensitive radio receivers, each with its own specially assigned tone code. A powerful centrally located transmitter broadcasts signals to all pagers in its area. But only one pager—the one assigned to the unique code pattern being transmitted—can hear it. When it hears its code, it springs to life: *BEEP*.

Most pagers fall into one of two categories: tone-only and tone and voice.

Tone-only was the original pager type and still represents more than half of all pagers in use. When someone wants to contact you, they dial a telephone number that corresponds to your pager. The phone rings at the paging company, and the transmitter automatically sends out the tone assigned to your pager and the pager responds by giving you a "beep, beep, beep." When you hear the beep, that's your signal to call the office, or wherever. Other pagers disregard the transmission.

For many people, tone-only pagers fill the bill, but for others, they just won't do. They need the added feature of voice paging. After beeping you, the transmitter stays on and allows the caller to send a short message over the phone to the person being paged. ("Harry, call your bookie.") Pagers usually have a 40- to 75-mile radius, much like a radio station, and because the receivers are extremely sensitive you often can be reached while walking in a building or driving in your car. Some people object to carrying pagers because they say it infringes on their privacy. Others use the pager's find-you-anywhere ability to grab a quick beer now and again while staying within reach of the office. After all, the caller doesn't know where you are when the beep goes off. Not yet, at least.

Although paging services saw a large boom in the mid-to-late 1970s, the industry has been fairly quiet since that spring day in 1950 when the first pagee was yanked off the golf green. Little had changed—until now.

For example, it used to be that if you travelled out of town with your pager you were out of range of your paging company's transmitter, and the pager was useless. But several paging companies now offer a reciprocal service: you borrow a pager from a company in the new city and either get a new temporary phone number or have your calls forwarded. That's okay if you're staying in a certain city for a couple of days, but what if you're constantly on the road? Until now, you would be incommunicado, as far as your pager was concerned.

But that's tame compared to what's new and what's coming. The once-simple pager is turning into a personal information-retrieval unit the likes of which were formerly only part of dreams or Star Trek episodes.

Nationwide Paging

In 1982, the Federal Communications Commission set aside for the first time special radio channels for nationwide paging, and companies immediately began to set up national paging networks. Now, you never have to change pagers or phone numbers or anything. One service called National Satellite Paging System uses the satellite network of public radio stations to beam its signals almost anywhere in the country. For example, someone dials your pager's local telephone number. The telephone number is recognized as one assigned for nationwide paging, and the call is automatically routed through the telephone system to Washington, D.C., the headquarters of National Public Radio. The call is sent to their satellite and relayed to all of the participating NPR stations. The signal is then sent via each station

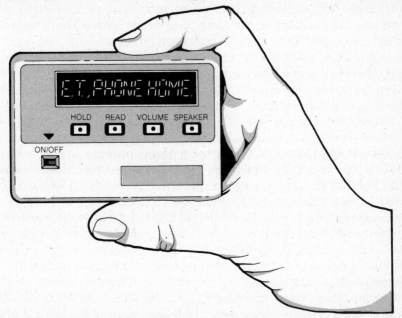

by telephone line to a local paging company. All over the country, your personal paging tones can be heard by millions of pagers, but only yours responds. Voila!

American Express, the credit card folks; MCI, the long distance phone company, which recently bought the paging company Airsignal; Metromedia, a broadcasting company; and Communications Industries, a radio manufacturer, also have joined forces to establish a 45- to 50-city paging system of their own. Instead of satellites, the consortium employs the MCI long distance network as well as the local Airsignal transmitters.

Because the initial target of national paging is business ex-

---

Dialing by Candlelight

Even during a power blackout, phone service works. Phones don't actually run on plug-in-the-wall electricity. Instead, phone service gets its juice from automobile-type storage batteries that are continuously charged by electricity from wall sockets. In case of a total power outage, batteries at the phone company can keep the nation's phone system working for about two days.

---

ecutives, American Express will use its experience catering to corporate officers to help market the new service. Of course, you can pay for the service through your credit card. The American Express pager: Don't leave home without it.

Right now, the nationwide paging systems handle tone only, but they will soon be able to offer voice. Before long, they will even serve the new crop of pagers now available locally that hold messages for customers without interrupting them. Instead of beeping you, the pager holds a message in its memory until you request it. Then, a small screen, like those on pocket calculators, gives you the message. It may be a phone number to call, a stock quotation, or a short sentence or two. These brand new devices can hold up to a thousand characters (numbers and letters), but with coming microchip technology that could be expanded to several pages of text. In addition, these bite-sized pagers offer priority alerts that warn you with a beep or strong vibration that an important message is coming in.

That's not all. On frequencies where voice paging is permitted, some paging companies offer call-store-and-forward services. For example, if a board meeting is set for Thursday at 3 PM, the secretary's office—which organized the meeting—merely calls a special number and leaves a voice message with a computer, which holds it in memory until the designated delivery date and time. In this case, board members' pagers may go off simultaneously at 1 PM on Thursday reciting the secretary's call, reminding them of the meeting two hours away. Messages may be stored up to 30 days in advance in many systems.

In addition, some pagers hold messages until a certain number of calls are logged, then beep the recipient to call in for messages. Or, it may hold all the recipient's messages until a certain time every day, as determined by the recipient, then rattle them off automatically. Some new models even have a microcassette

Telephones in the World's Major Cities
(Phones per 100 residents)

City	Phones	City	Phones
Amsterdam	75.7	Madrid	57.2
Atlanta	93.3	Manila	7.9
Auckland	55.1	New York	82.0
Berlin (West)	65.4	Oslo	86.5
Bombay	4.6	Ottawa	72.9
Boston	84.1	Paris	74.5
Brussels	66.7	Prague	50.7
Chicago	93.4	Rio de Janeiro	17.9
Copenhagen	85.4	Rome	53.8
Dublin	28.2	San Juan	47.9
Geneva	110.3	Santiago	9.0
Helsinki	89.2	Stockholm	125.1
Jerusalem	34.2	Sydney	58.4
Johannesburg	22.8	Tokyo	74.8
Lisbon	74.6	Vienna	63.6
London	79.3	Warsaw	29.2
Los Angeles	94.2	Washington	167.33

recorder attached to record incoming messages for later playback. The possibilities are endless.

There's still more. Not only can pagers readout onto screens, they also can print onto paper tapes. The units are a little bulkier than most pagers, about the size of a small tape recorder. They are aimed at salespeople and technicians who need lengthy instructional material such as inventory levels or data from the headquarter's main computer, but there is no reason why you can't call your spouse's pager and type in a last-minute grocery list.

International Paging

Some paging companies are beginning to develop international paging. PageAmerica/PageWorld Communications Inc. of New York City was the first to offer two-way paging services between several U.S. cities, London, and Tel Aviv. Ultimately, the firm hopes to have service available to Cairo, Geneva, Montreal, and 50 other foreign cities in Europe and Asia.

The system relies on reciprocal agreements between PageAmerica and overseas beeper companies. For instance, an American traveler in London would pick up a beeper (or, rather, "bleeper," as they call it in the U.K.) from Air Call Ltd., a British paging firm. Anyone trying to reach the global wanderer would dial a free "800" telephone number in the U.S., and the message would be routed directly to London, where our hero would be paged. The deal works the other way for a London-based traveler. With advances in direct-to-consumer satellites coming along swiftly, we may soon see international paging without the need to pick up new pagers as we travel. One pager will enable a message to reach you virtually anywhere in the world.

Most paging customers rent their pagers from companies known generically as "radio common carriers" (RCCs). Local telephone companies also supply paging services. Tone-only pager service runs about $15 to $20 per month. Voice pager service costs a bit more, about $25 a month. Some companies allow you to buy the pagers outright. Cost varies from $100 for a tone-only unit to $150 or more for a simple voice-only unit. To sign up, simply contact one of the many paging companies that serve your area.

When deciding which company to deal with, ask to see their coverage map. This will show you in what areas you can be reached. If you stay mostly in one area, you may save money by buying local service from a small RCC. But if you move around a larger territory you should choose a larger RCC, one with several transmitters linked together. Some RCCs cover several states.

Companies needing to contact their employees no matter where they roam within a local area have their own paging systems. Unlike a radio common carrier, they cannot sell their service to outsiders. If your company or organization needs its own paging system, contact the Federal Communications Commission's Private Radio Bureau for more information. If you show a bona fide need, they will assign a radio channel for paging. But be sure it is cheaper than using the services of a radio common carrier. Often, companies that already have permission to use the airwaves for two-way radio communications—such as hospitals and delivery services—can use the same channel for paging.

Another cheap way to get your own paging system is to use citizens band radio. You transmit a tone to turn on the pager, which is tuned to a CB frequency. Then, you send a voice message. The only drawback is that CB is limited to 5 watts, which means coverage of less than 10 miles. In addition, the CB band is very crowded in most areas, and you may have to wait for an available channel. Even so, any radio store that handles CB gear can probably get you going for less than $200.

Pagers use rechargeable batteries, and when you get your unit

Coin Telephones, by State

New York	210,455	Kentucky	16,919
California	187,454	Iowa	16,013
Texas	107,158	Kansas	15,531
Pennsylvania	100,006	South Carolina	15,474
Illinois	97,078	Mississippi	14,667
New Jersey	86,990	Arkansas	14,467
Florida	69,407	Oregon	11,784
Massachusetts	67,732	District of Columbia	11,021
Michigan	66,834	West Virginia	10,457
Ohio	64,380	Rhode Island	9,631
Maryland	40,515	Utah	8,265
Virginia	38,899	New Mexico	8,004
Georgia	35,692	New Hampshire	7,997
Indiana	31,558	Nebraska	7,062
Missouri	31,436	Maine	6,896
Tennessee	26,995	Montana	6,276
Wisconsin	25,678	Idaho	5,880
Connecticut	24,939	Hawaii	5,877
Louisiana	24,146	Delaware	5,407
Colorado	22,623	South Dakota	4,574
Oklahoma	20,671	Nevada	4,382
Alabama	20,104	Vermont	4,019
Washington	19,623	North Dakota	3,383
North Carolina	19,183	Wyoming	3,346
Arizona	19,160	Alaska	599
Minnesota	17,450		

it should come with a charging base into which the pager fits. It can be run while it's in the base, or you can turn the pager off, at night perhaps, and let it recharge for the next day's use. If you drive a great deal, the paging company can supply you with a wire and plug to fit into the cigarette lighter socket. Also, you may connect your pager to an outside car antenna for help in areas where reception may be marginal.

Even FM radio stations are getting into the paging act. For years, FM stations have transmitted background music on an unused part of their channel known as the "subcarrier." That's how they send a service widely known as "Muzak." You can't tell if the station you're listening to is transmitting on its subcarrier unless you have a special decoder device on your radio.

FM stations discovered they could send more than music on their subcarriers. Some use it to send tone-and-voice paging signals as well as stock market and commodity information. One

company, Telemet America Inc. of Arlington, Virginia, offers
subscribers in about a half-dozen cities a pocket calculator-type
device that gives them the latest stock quotes at the press of a
button. Want the latest IBM price? Press the letters I-B-M and
wait a few seconds. It pops up on the little red screen. If you're
following a hot stock, set your little paging device to beep when
it hits a certain price. Then call your broker and hope that if he
is out of the office, he took his pager.

CALLING ALL CARS, BOATS, AND PLANES

Having a telephone in your car may be classy, but up until now, it has also been frustrating. Even the most important executive has had to wait patiently for a clear radio channel before wheeling and dealing from a limousine. More than half the calls the exec wants to make won't make it through on the first try. There simply have not been enough channels for everyone who wants a car phone.

In New York City, for example, where New York Telephone operates one of the city's several mobile phone services, 700 customers have shared a measly 12 channels. That means only 12 conversations could take place at a time; the other 688 customers had to keep their dialing fingers on hold.

Although some 160,000 mobile telephones exist nationwide, more than 50,000 people have placed their names on waiting lists. In addition, phone company officials say that perhaps as many as ten times that number would jump on the bandwagon if they believed they had more than a slim chance for their own phone-on-the-go. Government officials estimate that more than a half-million people would request mobile service if they could get it immediately.

Once you understand how a conventional mobile phone service works, you can see why it was doomed to fail. Each major city has one, sometimes two, powerful transmitters to communicate with all car phones in a 30- to 50-mile radius. To make a call from your car, you must find a vacant channel, then call the operator and supply the phone number you want to call. The operator dials the number and connects you when the party answers. Some companies do provide dial-it-yourself service, but that's less common than operator-assisted service.

If someone wants to call you, they must first call the mobile operator for the city you are in. The operator finds a vacant channel and transmits a series of tones that correspond to your phone and make it ring—sort of as if it were a pager. (Again, some services use direct dial, but not many.) Once you answer, the operator connects you and the caller.

Clearly, the system is slow. Worse, it can't serve more than a dozen customers at a time, because the transmitter needs one channel for each call, and others within the transmitter's enormous operating range must wait their turn. During rush hour, it's almost impossible to get a call through anywhere near a major city.

The present system can't grow to accommodate more people unless many new channels are allocated, but that's impossible because frequencies in that portion of the radio band are scarce. So, mobile telephone companies are forced to limit the number of customers they serve, and you can't even get a mobile phone in many major metropolitan areas unless someone else gives up a unit first. It's a mess.

That's where a new system called "cellular mobile radio" comes to the rescue. This state-of-the-art system acts just like a regular land-based phone network. Millions of callers can use it at once without waiting and without operator assistance.

Because it acts just like a regular phone, you call anywhere in the world from your car, even to cars in other countries where cellular systems exist. Moreover, it's cheaper and more reliable than present mobile phone systems. Instead of only one or two powerful transmitters per region, an area is divided into many small sections called "cells." Each sports its own low-powered transmitter just strong enough to serve the cell. An average cell covers anywhere from one to eight square miles and varies in shape from a near perfect circle to something resembling a deflated, squashed football. Each cells touches each other; some overlap slightly.

Adjacent cells use different channels—there are more than 600 in each city to choose from—and a channel may be reused several times in each city if the cells are far enough apart. All the cells' transmitters hook into one network switching office, much like a central office handles calls from land-based telephones.

Each cell transmitter constantly sends out a special signal, and as you drive from cell to cell, your telephone automatically tunes in the strongest signal that it hears. When a call comes in for you, the network switching office uses the channel to send a signal containing your unique code number. Actually, it's a digital pulse that corresponds to the normal ten-digit phone number (area code plus seven-digit number) of your mobile phone.

When your unit hears its phone number, it in effect responds to the cell transmitter, "Here I am, in this cell." That information is relayed back to the network switching office, which scans its list of vacant voice channels and assigns one for your conversation. Then it relays that information to your cell transmitter. Finally, your unit tunes to that voice channel and the cell site rings you. You lift the phone and talk.

If this seems complicated, it is. But keep in mind this is all done automatically in seconds, without you even knowing it except for a small red light on your phone that lets you know you are within a working cell. Consider it your signal that you have a dial tone. Anyway, all these back-and-forth operations take only a few seconds, and when someone calls you they wait no longer than

A CELLULAR MOBILE RADIO NETWORK

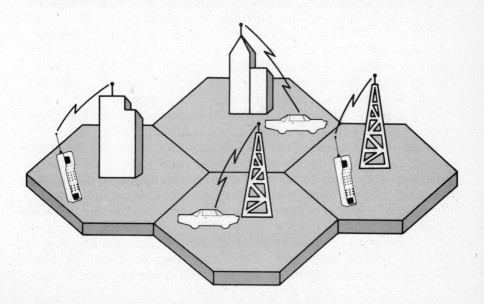

if they were calling a land-based phone. If you're already talking
on the line, they get a busy signal; if not, they hear a ring.

Making a call from your car is as simple as using a regular
Touch-Tone phone. You dial the number you want, and the computer goes through the same procedure but in reverse. You hear
a ring, and when your party answers, you pick up the handset
and talk. If their line is busy, you can call back later the easy
way. Most cellular phones remember the last number called and
you can dial it by pressing only one button. Many phones also
include a memory for up to ten frequently called numbers, so you
can dial them at a touch of a button, without taking your eyes
off the road.

Unlike present mobile phones, which often flutter and fade when
you travel too far from the transmitter, cellular radio transmissions are always strong, no matter where you drive in the cell.
And, as you drive from cell to cell, the computer at the network
switching office senses it and immediately "hands you off" to
the new cell. Neither you nor the party you're talking to notices
any change at all.

Even if you travel out of your area code region, you can still
keep a dial tone in your Dodge. As the system grows, you will
be able to initiate and receive calls from anywhere in the country.

The best part of it all is that as more mobiles are added to the
system, cells can be subdivided into still smaller cells without
crowding the airwaves. There is virtually no limit to the number
of mobile telephones that a system can handle.

Cellular mobile radio service already exists in Japan, Denmark,
Norway, and Sweden. In Denmark, service began in 1981 and
grew to 100,000 customers almost overnight. Within a few years,
all of Scandinavia will have compatible cellular systems.
Australia, Canada, and Mexico also plan systems.

The U.S. has lagged behind mainly because of government red
tape. The Federal Communications Commission studied the situation for almost twelve years before okaying the service in 1982.
Almost before the ink was dry on the final order, hundreds of
companies applied for licenses all over the country. If cellular
becomes the boom that everyone expects, the U.S. could be totally
"celled" by 1988. Imagine driving across the country in your own
phone booth!

The divested Bell companies plan service under the name
Cellular Service Company. Other companies such as GTE and
MCI plan similar services. Many radio common carriers are

Listening In

If you're one of the millions of Americans who owns a scanner radio to listen in on police and fire calls, you can check up on your local phone company repair trucks, installers, and linemen, too. Although the radio channels phone companies use vary from area to area, most are assigned one or two of the following frequencies: 151.985 (most common), 35.16, 42.16 (mobile), 158.34, 451.175 – 451.275, 451.3 – 451.675, 456.175 – 456.275 (mobile), 456.300 – 456.675 (mobile), 462.475, 462.525, 467.475 (mobile), 467.525 (mobile). Also, if you want to eavesdrop on callers using conventional mobile phone service, try these frequencies: 158.07 – 158.49 for mobiles and 152.81 – 153.03 for base stations. (All frequencies are in MegaHertz, or MHz.) Remember: It's against the law to divulge the contents of any conversations you may hear, but it's okay to listen.

prepared to build systems as well. Even companies outside the telecommunications industry, such as the Washington Post Company, the newspaper publisher, plan their own systems. Everyone wants a piece of the cellular service market, which is expected to serve three million customers by the end of the decade.

Already, two systems, one in Chicago and one in the Washington/Baltimore area, play to rave reviews from several thousand customers. Customers in Chicago pay between $45 and $60 a month to rent their phones, plus a $25 monthly usage fee for 120 minutes of airtime and 25 cents per minute thereafter. Bills average about $150 a month, and business customers say it is worth it. Salesmen claim they miss fewer calls, and executives say it turns an hour of commuting time into an hour of working time.

As the system grows, technology gets cheaper and competition becomes keener, monthly fees will plummet and may become as cheap as home phone service. Mobile phones, which now cost more than $1,000, could sell for less than $300 once in full production.

The main unit mounts in the trunk, and just the handset sits up front. Because it uses very high frequencies, the antennas are very small—about nine inches long—and can usually be hidden inside the car itself. Each unit contains a private code number that activates the phone, so when you park your car someone can't hop in and make long distance calls on your tab. By the way, the same computer that routes your phone call also prints up your monthly bill.

Besides mobile units, several companies also produce pocket-sized telephones that you carry. They work the same way as mobile units. They weigh about two pounds, a little heavy to actually keep in your pocket, but most of that bulk is because of rechargeable batteries. If battery technology progresses to the point where we get the same power with much less weight, the Dick Tracy wrist radio becomes a cartoonist's fantasy no longer.

In cars, cellular mobile units may replace two-way radios. Picture a plumber out on a service call. The dispatcher calls him on the regular office phone, and gives him the location of a panicked customer with a clogged drain. The plumber then calls the customer from his truck, perhaps asks a few questions about the problem, and tells him when he expects to arrive. If the plumber gets lost, he calls back for directions.

Or how about this one: cellular pay phones trucked in especially for outside concerts or fairs. A local company simply motors in banks of these cellular mobile equipped booths. It's easier and safer than stringing up temporary wires.

In rural areas, some high-tech entrepreneurs expect cellular radio to be less costly than regular wired phones for those who live way out in the boondocks. It's expensive to put in miles of telephone poles for just a few customers. Even for those living in the city, there is no reason why a cellular radio can't be your regular home or office phone as well. Nobody says a phone must be plugged into the wall anymore. And if you want to take it with you, you can. You will never miss a call.

Ahoy, Operator

Although mobile cells can easily be extended to include rivers and bays near cities, those further out in the ocean must still contend with conventional marine telephone systems. The system works similarly to mobile communications, but instead of the channels being jammed during morning and evening rush hours, rush hour takes place on sunny weekends.

To call someone on a boat, you must know what city they are near and the name of the boat. Most major coastal cities have marine operators, usually employed by the local phone company. Check with your local operator for the marine operator in the city nearest the boat.

The marine operator calls the boat on Marine Channel 16, which is reserved for calling and distress use only. If the boat is monitoring that channel, it will be instructed to switch to one of the nine channels set aside for marine telephone service. Very often, a boat must wait in line behind others receiving calls. Once the line is free, a marine operator connects the two parties together.

For a boat to initiate a call, it simply calls the marine operator on Channel 16 or one of the marine telephone channels. The operator than dials the number for you, and when the party answers the conversation begins on one of the telephone channels. Marine telephone services charge about a dollar or so plus the land-line call.

Buying a marine telephone for your boat is a snap because it's not a special piece of gear. It's a marine VHF (very high frequency) transceiver, which is used not only for marine telephone calls but for ship-to-ship and ship-to-shore use.

You can also buy hand-held marine radios. Weighing less than a pound, these walkie-talkies are great for keeping in touch while you're down below cleaning the bilge or topside sipping a cool one on the aft deck. Some of the newer hand-held models can send and receive on all marine channels, including those used for marine telephone service. But, unlike their full-sized counterparts, their power is low—usually less than 3 watts—and that limits their range to only a few miles.

Although there are more than 80 channels available for marine use, you won't need them all. Besides Channel 16—the calling and distress channel—which all transceivers have installed, find out from a local marine radio store which channels are used in your area. Store personnel also can instruct you how to obtain the proper FCC license needed before operating the radio.

Some channels are set aside strictly for commercial use while others are commonly used for pleasure craft to communicate ship-to-ship or ship-to-shore. Still others may be set aside, by local convention, for yacht clubs, yacht charter companies, gas stations, or harbormasters. Depending upon how busy your local marine operator is, you may not even need all the channels set aside for marine telephone service. Find out which channels your marine operator uses.

Unfortunately, those on the high seas cannot use their VHF radios to call the marine operator because the distances are too great. And, quite often, the long-range radios they do have can't make the haul because of adverse atmospheric conditions. For them, satellites are the only way to go.

As of February 1982, dialing ships at sea is easy sailing. More than 1,300 boats—ocean liners, tankers, private yachts—can be reached from any phone. The call is relayed by a marine satellite network known as INMARSAT, short for International Maritime Satellite.

If you want to wish your sister luck on her honeymoon cruise, make believe you're calling internationally, except you'll be dialing an over-the-seas (but not overseas) number; the country code is replaced by an ocean code.

Dial the international access code + ocean code + 7-digit ship ID number + the "#" symbol found on Touch-Tone phones. So, a call to a ship on the Atlantic Ocean becomes: 011 + 871 + 7-digit ship ID number + #. For the Pacific Ocean use 872 and for the Indian Ocean use 873. Just like in regular international direct dialing, the # symbol helps to speed the call through.

If your local telephone company isn't equipped for direct international dialing, call the operator and say: "I wish to place a call via INMARSAT," and when asked what country you want, give the proper ocean code and the ship's ID number or name. Advise the operator if it is a person-to-person call, collect call, or credit card call. Note that many ships request that their ID numbers be unpublished, just like asking for an unpublished number for your home phone. In those cases, an operator must honor that request. However, in a bona fide emergency, everything possible will be done to complete the call.

For direct-dial calls, costs average about $10 per minute plus charges from your phone to the coast station that beams your call to the satellite. There are three of those; two on the east coast and one on the west coast.

You can also send a Telex to INMARSAT-equipped ships. An international record carrier can supply the details on those calls.

Dialing the Friendly Skies

Although some crafty entrepreneurs tried attaching satellite dishes to airplanes—so they could use the INMARSAT system for making phones calls from the air—it just didn't work. The dishes kept blowing off. But not to worry: Telephone technocrats are wiring the friendly skies with airborne phone booths.

A company called AirFone Inc. has developed a system that allows you to make direct-dial calls from your airplane seat. You simply take out your credit card, insert it into the AirFone unit slot, pick up the handset, and dial the number you want. You are billed through your credit card company. If you don't have a credit card, you may buy a "cash card" from the airline.

AirFone charges a flat rate of about $7.50 for the first three minutes and $1.25 for each additional minute. The rate stays the same no matter where you call, no matter what the distance. You can dial coast-to-coast or anywhere in between. Moreover, if you're on the ground at about 16 major airports, you can call while you're waiting for take-off.

There are drawbacks to the system, however. Until the network is fully developed, not all airlines will have them. And, on those that do, only flights in the country's midsection—on a swath from New York to Atlanta stretching westward—will have the phone. Although once you're connected you can call anywhere, you can't call *from* everywhere until the system expands.

Unlike cellular mobile phones, where you are "handed off" as you move from cell to cell, the AirFone system connects you with a cell furthest from your plane in the direction you're headed, but once you pass that cell site, the signal will begin to fade. You get a warning tone, telling you that it's about to happen, and you must redial if you want to continue your conversation. For most people that won't be a problem. The average business call lasts about five minutes, and AirFone supplies about a twenty-minute connection time for each call.

To cut down on disruption in the cabin, only outgoing calls are allowed. You can't receive calls, because that means a lot of paging, and the airlines nixed the idea. Besides, cabin attendants have enough to do without adding telephone operator to their list of duties. How many telephones and how they will be distributed around the cabin is up to each individual airline. Some may pro-

vide phones to each row of seats and others may decide to install
several phones at the rear of the plane. Either way, once you slide
your credit card into the phone unit, you take the handset to your
seat and talk; it's cordless. You may also connect the phone to
a computer terminal to send or receive data.

In addition, there are plans afoot for customers to buy their
own air-phones and bring them on board. Once you leave the plane
you can't use it for calls until you are back at your home or office. Then it becomes a cordless phone by plugging the base into
a wall socket, just like any other cordless phone.

Who knows? Maybe one day you'll just need one phone
wherever you go—land, sea, or air.

DIALING FOR DATA

If a computer answers, don't—repeat, don't—hang up.

As it turns out, computers, which automatically answer phone calls with a high-pitched hum, may have more interesting things to say than some of your friends, and better gossip to tell than the yenta down the block. In fact, with the right equipment, it's possible to use your telephone for everything from banking and shopping to library research and stock portfolio management. And, of course, good gossip.

The arrival of small "personal" computers has meant the proliferation of all sorts of data bases, as what was once called "the office of the future" creeps quietly into the home of today. All of a sudden, there's more than just nagging voices and bill collectors on the other end of the line: The phone can provide direct access to virtually any source of information, opening up new possibilities for working—and playing—at home.

Hooking up to a computer via your telephone is done with a "modem" (short for MOdulator/DEModulator). Simply put, a modem is used to carry the computer's "voice" over the phone lines to converse with other computers.

Without getting too technical, suffice it to say that the modem converts the digital pulses produced by a computer into audio tones, which in turn can be transmitted over the phone. At the other end of the line, another modem reconverts these tones back into digital pulses.

The information is hardly transmitted in a flash, though. A typical modem used with a home computer will transmit data at

300 bits per second (300 "baud"), roughly equivalent to 30 characters per second, or about three-quarters of a minute for a page of double-spaced text. If the data is sent too fast, any noise on the line will garble the transmission. There are expensive, high-speed modems, however, that can handle data at 1200 baud, but they're generally out of the price range of home hobbyists. There are even souped-up modems that run at 9600 baud, but they won't do you much good because regular phone lines can't yet transmit data that fast without making errors.

Basically, there are two types of modems, direct-connect and acoustic couplers, both of which need to be plugged into an AC wall socket for power. The direct-connect modem plugs directly into your computer and telephone, while the acoustic model uses rubber cups into which the telephone handset is placed. Acoustic couplers traditionally have been cheaper than direct-connect modems, but are more sensitive to nearby noise, increasing the possibility of losing data during a transmission. This doesn't happen often, but it's an obvious consideration when shopping around. A 300-baud modem generally ranges from $100 to $200; models with extra features—such as dialing your phone automatically—cost a bit more.

Using the telephone and a modem to tap into data bases is a fairly simple matter. It can, however, become an expensive habit because of access charges and, in some cases, long distance costs. While some commercial services require a one-time sign-up fee, others charge only for a user's actual time "on line." Frequently, there will be different rates for on-line time, with normal business hours more expensive than evening or weekend hours.

In some cases, a full-blown home computer isn't even necessary to call data bases. Some of the cheaper models now on the market, including hand-held computers, have the capacity to communicate with other computers. In addition, there are "dumb" terminals which, unlike computers that can store and manipulate data, do nothing more than search certain data bases and retrieve the desired information. A few vendors even supply customers with special terminals—for a fee, of course—to tap into their services. And some of the business-oriented services have required courses to familiarize users with the intricacies of their systems.

Although commercial services—both for home and business use—may be located halfway around the country, phone bills need not necessarily be astronomical. Telenet and Tymnet are two of the more popular data communications networks that provide

What's a Digital?

Simply put, it's the opposite of an analog. More technically, a digital signal is one composed of electrical pulses that only have two states—on or off. If you had someone say "hello," and recorded all the usual ups and downs of their voice on tape, that's called "analog." If you took that same spoken word and divided it into very small pieces, each bit representing only one tiny part of that "hello," then took those pieces and recorded each one, that would be "digital." One way to visualize it is to look at a digital watch. Instead of the minute hand continuously going around, a digital watch "stops" time every second. It breaks the hour into discrete parts, each a minute long.

So what good is digital? For one thing, it's very accurate. Witness the digital watch: It's no longer "about a quarter to one," it's "twelve-forty-five, and thirty-eight seconds." More important, you can compress digital signals—squeeze them together—and send them over special telephone wires much faster than regular analog voice. All computers transmit digital pulses. That's why you need a modem. Regular telephone lines don't handle digital signals very well, so a modem takes the computer's digital pulses and converts them to analog before sending them over the phone lines. At the other end, another modem turns them back into digital so the receiving computer can read them.

local phone numbers for users of many computer networks. In effect, they work like WATS lines, allowing you to call a computer in a distant location for a fraction of the normal cost. By rerouting your local call to a distant computer over leased long distance lines, over which they send a great deal of data simultaneously, companies such as Telenet and Tymnet can save you considerable sums of money. There is, of course, a charge for these services, but it is modest compared to what a comparable long distance call would be.

In many cases, the type of data base right for you—particularly if your interests are specifically business or academically related—will be obvious. In other cases, though, it's going to take some shopping around and studying the lists of possibilities that each service offers. And even if you decide not to take the plunge and spring for a computer—the experts are betting, however, that you probably will before the end of the decade—you can still make good use of these services.

In addition to businesses popping up around the country which, for a fee, will search virtually any data base, university libraries are now routinely hooking up with major vendors. All libraries have different policies concerning who is eligible for having searches done. If you're doing any sort of serious research, where a computer search could mean days of library work done in minutes, look hard and long for a sympathetic librarian.

But if a home computer is on your shopping list, and you want to know specifically what will be available via the telephone, rest assured there's more than you've ever imagined. And, as we said, it's easily accessible by phone.

Going To The Source

The two most popular networks geared for the home user are CompuServe Information Service, a subsidiary of the H&R Block Company, and The Source, a subsidiary of Reader's Digest. These two services, which differ somewhat in the type of information they make available, offer everything from bridge and book reviews to stock quotes and ski conditions. Among the menu of choices available is everything from the useful to the you-think-I'm-going-to-pay-for-that? category: There's information on the latest in computer equipment, news, movie reviews, and classified advertising from a number of newspapers; electronic mail and banking; health and fitness advice; car care, college planning, and cattle prices. There's news from the federal government, games, gardening advice, sports, weather, recipes, rebate offers, airline schedules, and adult education.

And that's not the half of it. There's also African weather, baseball scores, defense news, grain futures, home decorating tips, an intelligence test, job listings, nutritional analysis, over-the-Counter stock prices, pilot information, real estate news, shop-at-home services, tax advice, video information, and news from such services as the Associated Press. CompuServe subscribers pay a one-time initiation fee, and are billed by the hour for their time on the system. (Rates for prime time—business hours—are higher than for evening and weekend hours.) Users receive a personal identification number and a password, which guards against someone running up your tab. At the end of the month, you're billed for time "on line," and yes, credit card payments are just fine.

Calling CompuServe is done via Tymnet (unless it's a local call for you to its Columbus, Ohio computer), which costs an additional $2 an hour during off hours and $10 during prime time. When the connection is made, the computer asks for your identification number and password, and away you go.

The systems are easy enough to use, but since you pay by the hour ($5 per hour during non-prime time on CompuServe) it's smart not to dawdle. Say, for example, you wanted to send a message to a computer-equipped friend or business associate over "EMAIL," CompuServe's electronic mail service. When signing on, you're presented with a series of choices:

> **CompuServe Information Service**
> **1 Newspapers**
> **2 Home Services**
> **3 Business & Financial Services**
> **4 Personal Computing Services**
> **5 User Information**
> **6 Index**

If you had entered a "2," the next menu of choices would look like this:

> **HOME SERVICES**
> **1 Newspapers**
> **2 Weather**
> **3 Reference Library**
> **4 Communications**
> **5 Shop/Bank at Home**
> **6 Groups and Clubs**
> **7 Games and Entertainment**
> **8 Education**
> **9 Home Management**

Now you enter number "4," to give you the communications menu, which brings you closer to the EMAIL set-up:

> **COMMUNICATIONS**
> **1 Electronic Mail**
>   **(user to user messages)**
> **2 CB Simulation**
> **3 National Bulletin Board**
>   **(public messages)**
> **4 User Directory**
> **5 Talk to Us**

Enter number "1" and you're almost there:

Welcome to EMAIL, the user-to-user message system from CompuServe. EMAIL allows you to communicate with other users of the information service. Instructions and options are included on each page. You are prompted for all required information. If you are not sure of what to do, key H (for help) and receive further instructions.

Finally, by pressing "Enter," the last menu comes up to get you ready to read or write:

> **Electronic Mail Main Menu**
> **1 Read mail**
> **2 Compose and send mail**

And so it goes. Getting into the area of your choosing is simple (the conversation above takes less than 30 seconds when you get used to it), and there are some interesting and worthwhile areas to explore. You can make airline reservations, for example, or order theater tickets. Sports fans can have a field day, there is considerable business information, and there are some interesting educational possibilities.

But there are also some dangers—like not keeping track of your time on the system. There is also the question of whether you need to spend $22.50 an hour during prime time to test your prowess with trivia quizzes, or to get the answer to Rubik's Cube, both of which are available on CompuServe. You may, of course, also be billed for local message units by your phone company, and giving your password and identification number to the kids could be like giving your gasoline credit cards to your teenager.

Some of the services on CompuServe can also save you the cost of buying your own computer programs. FINTOL, for instance, is a set of computerized financial tools that can help you analyze such things as monthly mortgage payments at different interest rates or depreciation rates. Banking and shopping at home is possible, and another nice feature lets subscribers save personal information on CompuServe's computers, creating their own private files; there's a nominal monthly storage fee. It is also possible to have CompuServe print and mail your files to you for an additional charge.

The Source, which houses more than a thousand information and communications services, is in many ways similar to Compu-

---

PhonePhreaks

In the mid-1970s, cheating the phone company became the great national pastime among a select group of folks known as "PhonePhreaks." These hearty young souls knew more about the phone network than many AT&T engineers, and they learned most of it by reading AT&T technical journals and by experimenting with their own phones. Some of the original PhonePhreaks were blind college students who, because of their overdeveloped sense of hearing, could recognize and reproduce the unique telephone tones that would give them access to long distance lines and to make phone calls without tripping the billing mechanism. Their experiments led to the famous "blue box," a device that gave any caller the ability to phone free virtually anywhere in the world. The boxes could be built for less than $20, and AT&T, joined by local and federal law enforcement agents, raided blue-box users' homes and businesses. PhonePhreaks are still alive and well, but today they seem more interested in breaking computer networks then telephone networks. Some have banded together and operate under the name Technology Assistance Group.

Serve, although the start-up fees are somewhat higher. The Source has a full complement of business, financial, news, consumer, and communications files. It also has astrological forecasts, magic tricks, chess and checkers, restaurant reviews, ski resorts, and florists' phone numbers. United Press International (UPI) news is available, but unlike CompuServe, which has a number of newspapers on-line, The Source only has one, *The New York Times.*

Among its more interesting features is its electronic mail service, which has a "Chat" function that lets you talk directly over the keyboard to other users and print out the conversation. Voicegram is a service that lets you call a toll-free number and dictate a message of up to one hundred words, which can be sent to any other Source user or users.

The Source's Travel Club lets you be your own travel agent, scanning airline schedules, making hotel, plane, and rental car reservations. In addition to shopping on The Source, where you can see a catalog of Source-chosen products, complete with monthly specials, there is a barter network that lets subscribers cut their own deals. Through The Source you can tap into Computer Search International, a nationwide network of recruitment firms, and Musicsource, which lets you order records and audio and video tapes at discount prices, charging them to your credit cards. There's also a data base that teaches you how to order fine wines in a restaurant—just in case you can hang up the phone long enough to actually go out to dinner.

Getting Down To Business

Although services such as The Source and CompuServe can be of use to small businesses and individual consumers, there are companies geared exclusively for business or research applications.

Stock market watchers may be especially interested in the Dow Jones News/Retrieval service. Hooking up to this on-line service requires purchasing a moderately-priced program (under $50) for your computer. Time on the Dow Jones service is comparatively expensive—about $30 to $60 per hour, with additional charges for access to special files—but for those serious about their portfolios, it offers a chance to really play stock broker with a personal computerized "ticker tape." There is continuously updated stock price information for four U.S. stock exchanges: New York, American, Pacific, and Midwest. It is also possible to obtain current bond prices from three exchanges, options from four exchanges, over-the-counter prices, and updates on mutual funds and U.S. Treasury issues.

That's just the beginning. The service offers historical information, including stock price trends, historical quotes, and news developments on companies. Subscribers can search an enormous pool of articles from *The Wall Street Journal, Barron's* and the Dow Jones News Service. You can do a check on a specific company, or you can do a subject search, calling up articles on, say, magnesium mining for a specific year. You can view the findings on your screen or print them on your computer's printer (with some computers, you can store the material on a floppy disk for use at a later time). You can look at balance sheet items, quarterly income statements, specifics from corporations' annual 10-K forms, five-year income and earning summaries, and information about officers and directors of the corporation. And you can even order up recent transcripts of the popular Public Broadcasting Service program "Wall Street Week."

Among the other features that Dow Jones News/Retrieval offers is something called the Corporate Earnings Estimator, which provides a statistical summary of brokerage analyst earnings per share from top Wall Street firms, and the *Academic American*

Encyclopedia. Gone are the days of waiting for the annual en-
cylopedia yearbook: This reference work, which contains 28,000
articles, can be updated and edited whenever necessary. And, if
there's a pertinent article in the encyclopedia, a story in the
News/Retrieval data base—which, by the way, covers general interest news and weather in addition to financial facts—will make
reference to it.

If newspaper and magazine research is of importance, Nexis,
a service of Mead Data Central, will keep you happy. This data
base is patterned after Lexis, a legal and accounting research service that may leave judges and lawyers wondering if they really
need law clerks. Nexis users simply tell the computer that they're
looking for stories about any topic—or topics—and it will turn
up the entire texts (not just abstracts) of appropriate pieces.

Generally, Nexis carries newspaper and wire stories dating back
to January 1, 1977, and magazine articles from January 1, 1975.
Among the sources included in the data bank are Associated
Press, United Press International, Reuters, *The Washington Post,
Newsweek, Dun's Review, The Economist, U.S. News and World
Report,* the Public Relations Newswire, and *Congressional
Quarterly Weekly Report.*

As with most services of this sort, the time of day determines
the on-line cost, which generally runs between $1 and $1.50 a
minute. Nexis also includes newsletters in its data base, and con-
tinues to make additional publications accessible. And, unlike
many data bases, Nexis can be used only through special terminals supplied by the company. Any old home computer won't
do in this case.

Equally intriguing are two data bases that provide access to
hundreds of other data bases: Dialog and the Bibliographic
Retrieval Services.

Dialog, owned by Lockheed, the airplane people, is the granddaddy of this category, offering wide-ranging coverage of science,
technology, business, economics, social sciences, and engineering. The cost per minute varies, depending on the data base you
search, and it's possible to have the material you want printed
"off-line" and sent to you, thereby reducing your "on-line"
charges.

A lot of what Dialog has available is of limited interest, intended
more for researchers than for the general public. Among the data
bases available, for example, are summaries of all recent patents,
criminal justice abstracts, environmental and food science cita-

tions, sociological and psychological abstracts, Standard & Poor's news, statistics from the U.S. Commerce, Energy, and Labor Departments, and even a philosophy index.

In addition, it's possible to search the *Foundation Grants Index,* which contains information on grants awarded by more than 400 major American philanthropic foundations. *Federal Register* abstracts, dating back to March 1977, provide details of federal regulatory agency activities, including legal notices and proposed rules, references to meetings and hearings, and new public laws. There's also the *Book Review Index,* which maintains all reviews of books and periodicals from nearly 400 journals.

There is no start-up cost for the Dialog service; subscribers, who connect via Telenet or Tymnet, are billed only for on-line time, along with a small charge for each citation printed off-line.

There are additional services of Dialog to make your life a little easier. One service gives an automatic search of a subject you've chosen and alerts you every time new information comes in. Another service lets you order the full text of documents that turn up in your search only as abstracts.

BRS is similar in many ways to Dialog, although there is a different collection of data bases. The New York Times Information Bank is a handy research tool providing instant access to a number of newspapers across the country, including, of course, *The New York Times.* BRS also touts its very cheap nighttime service called "AfterDark," designed with the home user in mind.

A wide variety of newsletters are now available on-line through the Pennsylvania-based NewsNet, everything from *Fiber/Laser News* and *Coal Outlook Marketline* to *Cellular Radio News* and *Viewdata/Videotex Report.*

For the last word on what's available, consult the mammoth *Encyclopedia of Information Systems and Services* for a comprehensive review of all data bases. Ironically, it's not available on any computer.

Bulletin Boards

All over the country, computer stores and good samaritans have set up computerized bulletin boards (CBBs), which are, in effect, public electronic mail services. To tap into these boards, you simply call up, listen for the high-pitched hum (the "carrier signal"), and, with modem operating, away you go. It's just like using the commercial data services, but these, believe it or not, are free.

Of course, the adage about the worth of getting something for nothing is often appropriate. While some of the bulletin boards are set up for special interest use—astronomy, games, or medical information, for example—most merely allow callers to read and leave messages. Depending on the type of people using the boards, this computerized version of CB radio can provoke stimulating conversation or mindless chatter. Some CBBs have endless political debates going; others, as they get more sophisticated, and interest grows, are offering services such as discount shopping and free-for-the-taking computer programs. And, some people have found the bulletin boards a fine alternative to the personals column in many magazines—a free, interactive dating service. You can carry on conversations—voiceless conversations, that is—with would-be friends or lovers before deciding whether you actually want to meet.

Finding bulletin boards is easy—most computer stores can give you the number of a couple—and once on the board you're likely to see messages about other boards. Most boards are accessible by all makes of computers. There are even newsletters that list the whereabouts, phone numbers, and operating hours of bulletin boards across the country, and some bulletin boards have a comprehensive listing of other boards in your area—or even across the nation.

Most bulletin boards are "user friendly," meaning that instructions for using the system are given in plain, simple English. (Generally, directions can be found by hitting the "Help" command.) A typical board will allow you to leave messages—password protected if you like, so only specific individuals can view them—and read through messages that others left.

And how does it all work? Here's a typical—if somewhat abbreviated—real-life session with a CBB, offering a sample of the type of messages you might find.

In this case, Ralph Seidner, a computer enthusiast in Boston, calls a system in Washington, D.C. using his long distance phone service. Because this is a long distance call, Ralph may not want to linger: he can check the "D" file to see if his friends in Washington have left a password-protected message for him (no one else will be able to see it); he can check the "S" file for short summaries of messages to decide which he wants to read through; he can check the users' log to look for familiar names; and he can check "O" now and then to see how many minutes he has been on the line. Finally, Ralph can read through some of the

messages—and then decide if he might better spend his money
calling his mother in Florida. (Ralph's entries are in italic; all
messages are guaranteed verbatim, and guaranteed typical—at
least for the board they came from.)

Welcome to The Computer Mart's Bulletin Board System!
Type "I" for system information, "H" for help.
Please use system responsibly—KILL your old messages!
First Name? *Ralph*
Last Name? *Seidner*
Location? *Boston*
RALPH SEIDNER
Of Boston
Correct, Ralph? *Yes*
You are user # 16338

Messages in system: 1 thru 10, 12902 thru 13062
Total messages : 93
Command? *H*

Commands:

B (ulletin Board Numbers)
M (essages in system)
C (hange Linefeed switch)
N (ulls change)
D (isplay Password messages)
O (nline time)
E (nter message)
P (rompt on/off)
F (lagged message retrieve)
Q (uick summary)
H (elp with commands)
R (etrieve messages)
I (nformation about system)
S (ummary of messages)
K (ill a message)
T (erminate session)
L (ogon again)
U (sers' log)

Need more help (Y/N)? *Y*

Enter command you wish help with: /
"P" — pause, "S" — exit, "H" — help with another
comand.

The Information command will give data about the
system and things you need to know to best utilize it.
Please use this command if you have not previously
done so.

Enter command you wish help with: R

The retrieve command allows you to read messages. It
allows selective retrieval similar to selective summary.
It also lets you do a multiple retrieval (all messages
from a starting to an ending number) or individual
message retrieval. "S" typed while the message is
listing will return to command mode, "N" goes to the
next message, and "P" causes display to pause until
another character is struck. Graphics messages,
denoted by (G) in the subject, automatically pause at
the end of the message.

Command? R

Multiple retrieval? Yes
Selective retrieval? No
Start at # (1 - 10, 12902 - 13062): 12902
End at #: 13062

Msg : 12960 (K) Lines = 16.
Date: 10/01 17:18
From: Charlie Russo
To : All
Subj: micro encounters
friends, washingtonians, and countrymen, lend me your
ears. There is a new bbs up called microencounters. It
is exactly like the prince william county trs-bbs, which
is a forum 80 board. yet microencounters is charging
$50 just for a few months time on a boring board. call
it up folks and see for yourself. from what i saw it really is a ripoff. the source is cheaper in the long-run.
send your comments, good, or bad, to me.

Msg : 12988 (K) Lines = 2.
Date: 10/05 00:54
From: Amy Holsapple
To : All
Subj: Military Field Tables
IF ANYONE OUT THERE KNOWS WHERE I CAN OB-
TAIN ANY TYPE OF MILITARY FIELD TABLES PLEASE
LET ME KNOW.

Msg : 12996 (K) Lines = 3
Date: 10/05 16:16
From: FRED SCHMIDT
To : CHARLIE RUSSO
Subj: MICROENCOUNTERS
I'VE CALLED THE # AND "TALKED" TO A NICE
WOMAN. SHE WAS VERY PLEASANT AND WILLING
TO HELP ME. I DON'T SEE WHERE YOU GET IT AS
BEING A RIP-OFF. I FOUND IT EXCITING. SORRY TO
SHOOT DOWN YOUR HOT BALLOON!!

Msg : 13057 (K) Lines = 11.
Date: 10/14 12:28
From: Jerry Schoenholtz
To : Grippo
Subj: TRSBBS
I am sorry to hear that you have folded your system
up, although I can fully understand why. It does get to
be a pain to not be able to use your own equipment
because there is a caller on the system. The un-
appreciative crackpots who try to crash your system
and want to throw firebombs at your computer don't
increase your desire to keep it up. Again, I am gen-
uinely sorry to learn of its demise. Jerry

Msg : 13034 (K) Lines = 5.
Date: 10/10 16:15
From: Peter Goldwater
To : All
Subj: Food
GUESS WHAT!!!!! I JUST SPILLED SPAGHETTI ALL
OVER MY ATARI 800!!!!!!! DOES ANYONE KNOW
HOW TO EXPLAIN THAT TO THE REPAIR
TECHNICIAN?????

Msg : 13004 (K) Lines = 4.
Date: 10/05 23:12
From: Rufus Stein
To : All
Subj: Atari Computers
Anyone out there with an Atari, mine would love to talk to yours. Leave your number on this BBS. I will check back in a week.

Msg : 13057 (K) Lines = 8.
Date: 10/14 12:28
From: Jerry Schoenholtz
To : SYSOP
Subj: Messages
Except for the message prior to this one, I am not responsible for any other messages on this system. Please feel free to kill any and all messages that appear on this system either from me, to me, or about me - as I am not responsible for them. This also includes any messages that may be entered in the future. Please kill this message . Jerry

Msg : 13088 (K) Lines = 1.
Date: 10/18 19:04
From: Gary Prushansky
To : Christene Powers
Subj: punks
Where did all the punks go?

You get the idea. These boards, for the most part, are cluttered with computer talk, items for sale, and idle chatter; a bit of fun, but not much substance. Some boards, however, show the possibilites that the merger of the computer and the telephone—even in a not-for-profit situation—can bring about.

An example of a high-class board is one run by NASA in Greenbelt, Maryland. The Get-Away Special (GAS) Program, which offers the opportunity to get an experiment aboard the Space Shuttle, has a users' network (GAS-NET) to help with related questions. NASA officials will only answer inquiries from GAS experimenters, but anyone is free to monitor the board to get the inside track on what people are planning and the progress of upcoming missions.

A man in Rhode Island, for example, who wants NASA researchers to help him with his ideas for spacecraft propulsion, left the following message in the system:

I am currently doing some research in concentrating centrifugal force in one direction. I did a patent search and found one patent that may help me. The idea basically operates the same as Donald Cook's exchange of mass idea. There is one huge flywheel that rotates all the time. Inside this flywheel are mounted two gyros. Both of the inertial masses (smaller flywheels) on the gyros are also kept on all the time (call this the X-axis). If one should rotate one of the gyros on the Y-axis, a force will be generated perpendicular to the X-axis. However, let's say one of the gyros is only on during half cycle of the large flywheel. And the other gyro's motor that controls the Y-axis rotation is on the other half cycle of the large flywheel. Is it true that a force is concentrated along the 90 degree part of the large flywheel? If it is, then this force can be concentrated up and thus establish a lift. If this idea works then a propulsion system of this type can be used on the shuttle. This system of converting a mechanical energy into thrust is more efficient than the shuttle's current method of ejecting mass and giving off tremendous amount of heat. This system, if it works, hardly involves any heat, except for that of friction.

There is, in short, a lot of information on the other end of the line, some useful, some barely worth tracking down. As the home computer market grows, the number of data bases and bulletin boards undoubtedly will increase as well. This makes having the right phone equipment and services all the more important.

And if you're wondering whether all this has any real, practical value—or, for that matter, if using the phone lines for such novel things really works, consider the following: this book was written on the authors' home computers; the text was sent over the phone lines to our editor's computer; he, in turn, did his editing and sent the manuscript over the phone to the typesetter's computer, where it was set into type and printed out for the artist, who put it all together for the printer. And, yes, everything went without a hitch.

FUTUREGAB

Telephone trade association meetings are, for the most part, about as memorable as Mah-Jongg tournaments. In September 1979, however, in a speech to the annual fall conference of the National Telephone Cooperative Association, a vice president of AT&T detailed the coming technologies (most of which have since arrived), and then set the stage for the future with a truly memorable statement: "As far as the technology goes," he said, "the range of services that the network will be capable of providing is probably limited by the breadth of our imagination and inventiveness."

Indeed, the technology already exists for many of the services that we may envision as the ultimate in telephone equipment. But it may be years before many of these services are available, partly because demand is not yet great enough, prices are still too high, and the regulatory considerations have not been ironed out.

There are, however, indications of what will be available in the coming months and years. In fact, the first few waves of future-tech products and services already have rolled onto shore. If you think call waiting is a big deal now, hold the phone.

In many ways, the telephone will be the appliance around which our lives will revolve—the ubiquitous, take-it-with-you communicator that will allow us to do everything from turning on the stove an hour before we come home to voting without going to the polls. If the technology evolves the way some pundits predict, we'll routinely be spending more time on the phone—although not just in conversation with other humans—than two teenage lovebirds.

Fortunately, there will be at least some safeguards to protect our privacy and make life with Princess easier. Consider, for example, the telephone that either gives a digital readout of the number from which you're being called or arranges priority ringing signals, so you could tell who's calling before you answered (or didn't answer). Similarly, the technology probably will allow for programmable phones that will always be busy when called from designated numbers. Don't want to talk to your landlord? Just program your phone appropriately, and every time he calls (until he gets wise and heads for a phone booth) he'll get a busy signal.

Another problem for phone users is that while you're tying up your line in conversation, you never know if someone is trying to get through to you. Call waiting solves part of that problem, but presumably there are times when you don't want to interrupt a conversation to check on who is calling in. With the phone system of the not-too-distant future, your phone will be able to automatically call back the person who received a busy signal when calling you. (Of course, if it's the landlord that was trying to get through, you'll be able to program the phone not to return the call.)

Paging Mr. Orwell

Perhaps the most profound changes we'll see will result from the marriage of phones and computers. To some extent, this process has already started, particularly in the business community. But the long-term implications of these new-tech nuptials are enough to make some people want to go back to town criers and Dixie Cups connected with string.

The big change coming is the electronic home—the wired nation to the nth power. Under the scenario, which already is being tested by some corporations, people don't actually go to work but instead toil at home. In this world of telecommuting, work is done on the home computer, which is connected to the office by telephone. No more rush-hour traffic jams, no more needing to act civil on Monday morning, no more mindless gossip at the water fountains. No more people.

The video revolution and the telephone revolution are coming together to form a technological revolution that will have profound effects on our lives. With the ability of our televisions to receive both teletext (one-way information services) and videotext

Would I Lie To You, Boss?

One day you wake up, decide you'd rather not go to work, so you call the office. "Boss," you say in the hoarsest voice you can muster, "I don't feel well. I'm staying home." The boss is quiet, waits half a minute and says, "Listen, I know you're not really sick, but if you need a day off, take it. See you tomorrow." And hangs up.

It may be his intuition that made him wise or it may be his new Psychological Stress Evaluator (PSE), a lie detector that works over the phone. Nonsense, you say. Believe it; it's true.

Invented by two Army intelligence officers during the Vietnam War, it was designed on the same principle as the polygraph, what most people call the lie detector. With wires strapped to your wrists, chest, and other key locations, a polygraph senses subtle changes in your breathing, heart rate, and muscles when you are under stress—like when you are telling a fib.

The PSE works the same way, by sensing and comparing tiny voice changes called "microtremors," which occur in the human voice when a person is under stress. Unless you're a sociopath (who believes that what he says is always the truth even if it's not), the PSE works as well as a polygraph. It works on taped voices, too.

There is no law against using a PSE, and you can buy models ranging from suitcase-sized units to ones that fit into a cigarette pack. Prices range from several hundred dollars to several thousand dollars.

Like a polygraph, a PSE is not usually admissible as court evidence because there are too many variables involved in its use. Using it without knowledge of the subject may not be entirely illegal, although it certainly is unethical. Still, many law enforcement agencies routinely use them when talking by phone to snitches, bomb threateners, and others.

The largest user is private industry, however. Businesspeople believe it gives them a slight edge when negotiating contracts over the phone ("The PSE indicates that he'll come down several thousand dollars on the deal") or for other such strategic purposes.

So, the next time you need a day off from the office, don't say you're sick. Just say you're not coming in.

(interactive services), we'll have a wide range of information services at our disposal. Telephone wires are one of the principal ways these services will be delivered to the home, with the telephone/computer combination giving us the wherewithal for everything from banking transactions to electronic messaging; from games and entertainment to electronic directories and teleshopping.

But it won't be just a handful of consumers with home computers and subscriptions to commercial services like The Source.

Indeed, a 1982 study done for the National Science Foundation predicts that 40 percent of all American households will have some sort of teletext service by 1990, and around 30 percent will have two-way videotext service by the turn of the century. This, in short, will mean the real arrival of the electronic home information-entertainment-employment center, the place from which work is done by a significant percentage of the population—the place, in fact, where virtually everything is done. And the implications for the year 2000 are rather intriguing, says NSF: "In the electronic home, familial ties of interdependence may be based on new skills. Spouses may be drawn to each other as much for their ability to manipulate data bases as for their ability to prepare gourmet meals or to play racquetball." (Wanna come up to my place and check the commodity futures index?)

Other changes this revolution may bring are equally interesting:

- The dwelling unit (we still call it home) will become a place of employment. This not only affects its structure, in terms of architecture, and layout, but also its geographical location. In other words, where we live won't necessarily be determined by where we work or shop, or where our kids go to school.
- The electronic household will help create a new home-based cottage industry in electronic products. This has already begun, with small-time entrepreneurs making big-time fortunes creating and marketing computer software.
- Home-based shopping, along with computer-aided production, will allow us to control the manufacturing process. We will be able to order exactly what we want for "production on demand." A specific model toaster, for example—including a specific color and with specific options—can roll off the assembly line after it is ordered on the phone.
- The family will determine the electronic schooling required for children and for the retraining of adults. There will be a shift away from the traditional school and work socialization processes to ones in which peer groups and alliances are electronically determined. Computer-aided learning will allow each child's curriculum to be more specialized.
- New skills and career paths associated with management of information will emerge. These will range from information brokers who locate the "best" deal on a used car to information gatekeepers who monitor political and corporate ac-

---

We All Make Mistakes

After many attempts to get his invention to operate clearly over long distances, pessimism overtook Alexander Graham Bell and his partners. They were ready to give up and offered the rights to the telephone to Western Union Telegraph Company in 1876 for a mere $100,000. It's not certain why the president of Western Union refused. Historians suggest it was because he thought Bell's company was pulling a fast one, trying to sell them a useless product.

---

tivities and release this information to those parties who are interested.
- There will be an increase in opportunities to participate in educational, social, and political arenas. This will happen as the interactive capacity of the new media allows greater involvement of the public. You'll not only be able to vote by telephone-linked computer, you'll also be able to express your opinion on issues with the push of a few buttons.

In short, the future holds more for the telephone than merely ordering pizzas. The widespread acceptance of teletext and videotext will mean the true electronic cottage, with those wires in our homes bringing in and sending out a wide variety of audio, video, and text. If it all sounds terrific, consider this prediction from the National Science Foundation report:

The interaction with elected representatives has many new aspects. A computer clearinghouse (electronic ombudsman) receives and investigates complaints against the government and its agencies. Individuals have an electronic means of contacting and possibly influencing decision-makers who in turn can respond on a personal basis. Public opinion polls are much more extensive and timely and the results are available at many levels: household; age group; income group; type of employment. Access, though ostensibly universal, becomes available to the privileged or those prepared to pay. Citizens who lodge complaints may find that their electronic profile of past political involvement is exposed. The protection of citizen rights and protection of privacy are of key concern.

Practically Practical

That scenario, of course, is turn-of-the-century speculation, but parts of that scenario—the good parts—are already history. In 1982, for example, one member of Congress began a two-way electronic message system between his Washington office and his Pennsylvania district, all using phone lines.

Using CompuServe's EMAIL system, Representative James Coyne's constituents could call a local number in the Philadelphia area and enter a message on their home computers. The messages would be saved in Coyne's computer "mailbox," allowing him to retrieve and answer these messages at his convenience. Using this type of system, constituents don't have to rely on traditional mail service, which would take a few days at best. And for a member of Congress, an immediate response can be sent to a constituent via the office computer. Will the home computer and the telephone increase Americans' participation in government? It's too early to tell, but the technology makes it possible.

So far, electronic mail is still used almost exclusively by business, but the pundits believe that will change. They also believe its use, the ideal antidote to "telephone tag," will expand rapidly by both business and home users. One recent study, for example, predicts that around a million people will send more than 11 billion electronic messages annually by 1995, compared with fewer than a billion such messages sent by only 160,000 people during 1982.

The prototype of what you may have in your home one day is already on some desks in offices around the country. The plain black phone—or even the Pac-Man phone—will give way to what looks like a small computer terminal, complete with keyboard and screen. These terminals can be used at home—and are ideal for the person running a home-based business—or can be hooked into larger office systems. They're not as complicated to use as today's home computers, but have many of the features of a microcomputer. A "Help" key, for example, will give assistance if you get into a jam.

The Ultimate Phone?

As for the "standard" telephone of the future, a prototype has arrived.

DataVoice, manufactured by Basic Telecommunications Cor-

Infinity is a Long, Long Distance

The well-dressed wiretapper simply wouldn't go out without an infinity transmitter. A cute little number, this cube-shaped beauty sits inside your telephone and doesn't disturb a thing. But when your phone is dialed and the caller sends the proper tone (a whistle or correct Touch-Tone sequence will often do), the infinity transmitter stops your phone from ringing and activates its own microphone. The surreptitious soul can then hear everything in the room, even though the phone is still on the hook. Neat.

The device costs about $500, and you can buy it at any number of electronics stores, which sell them under the guise of such legal gizmos as a remote baby sitter. (Hey, Jimbo, call and check on the kid, why-don't-ya.) It can't listen in on phone calls, however.

poration, carries the label of "telephone," but it's really a "desktop communications system." DataVoice is designed for business use, but a company spokesman says he sees future-generation models being designed for home use. You may not presently need all the functions the unit makes available, but some day you may. And here's what you'll get for your money:

DataVoice looks like a computer terminal. It has a nine-inch screen and a full-size typewriter-style keyboard attached to the unit with a coil cord. Of course, there's also a standard telephone handset for saying hello and a keypad for dialing. With this little wizard, you can send data and voice messages to any other location—even when you're not actually near the phone—at any time you want. In addition, it will automatically receive voice and data messages when you're not there. (The souped-up model has a built-in cassette recorder, which lets you tape voice and data directly and store it for safekeeping.)

DataVoice has a built-in modem, which lets you tap into virtually any data base you can dial. It has a word-processing function, meaning you can edit your messages before sending or storing, and a 200-year calendar/appointment book that will remind you when it's time to place a call, meet the boss, or plan your retirement, decades hence. It's got a built-in phone directory that automatically alphabetizes your entries, and you never actually have to dial a number fully, since DataVoice does it for you with the push of a button. It's got a "Help" key to explain how to work the thing in case you forget, and it's set up to connect directly to a printer. With that little extra, you can get access to The

Source or CompuServe and print out the data you're looking for directly; print out your messages; or print out your schedule for the coming week. It's about the size of a small typewriter, it's got a battery backup in case there's a power failure, and it's possible to hook up floppy disk drives for maximum storage capacity. All for about $2,500.

The Ultimate Phone Line?

And while the present telephone system won't be outmoded for many years, futurists have already begun work on the phone line of the future.

It's called the Integrated Services Digital Network (ISDN), and the standards are now being developed. The theory behind ISDN is that all electronic communications—voice, data, and video—will come into your home through one electronic "pipeline." This theoretically will give you more flexibility in merging various technologies, more ease in hooking up new hardware, and presumably, cheaper prices for these services.

Implementation of ISDN probably won't begin until at least the early 1990s. When such a system is in place, though, you will benefit substantially. The main applications, in addition to voice and video, will be such things as interactive data and electronic mail, security and fire alarms, and facsimile transmissions, which will allow the easy and rapid transmittal of documents from one point to another. This means you'll be able to go into an appliance store, buy any communications equipment you need, take it home and plug it in. No more installation or hook-up fees, and a near-complete merger of all modes of electronic communications.

This single pipeline will make life a bit easier, but many of the technologies that will be integrated in the network will be available years before ISDN is a reality. Already, consumers and small businesses in many parts of the country are relying on their phone company for enhanced security services that monitor the premises for intruders, fire, floods, or power failures.

An experiment going on in Germany may also offer a peek into things to come. The Federal Post Office has contracted to have "Bigfon" islands installed in two cities by 1983. The limited test will give home subscribers access to such services as Picturephone, interactive videotext, Telex, and a variety of radio and television programs. Subscribers with Picturephone service will be able to see who they're talking to via their TV screens.

Whether residential Picturephone service will ever be standard here is mostly a matter of whether the public wants it (and is willing to pay the price), rather than whether it's technologically feasible. Either way, you will soon be able to have a phone that, at the very least, will be tied into the telephone company's computer, giving you options such as data storage and retrieval. The phone will monitor energy usage in your home or business, let you take part in audio and video teleconferences, and let you read your favorite publications without actually buying them on the newsstands.

Ultimately, the telephone will be merely another piece in an overall system of communications components. But instead of being anchored in your home or at your desk, it will go with you: the Walkman of tomorrow will be a two-way affair. In fact, some predict that the Timex on your wrist will eventually be able to send and receive calls worldwide.

Dick Tracy probably wouldn't even flinch at such a prospect, but Alexander Graham Bell simply wouldn't believe it.

INDEX

The

YELLOW PAGES

How to Use The Yellow Pages

Simply look up the telephone, accessory, or service you are interested in. With a few exceptions, companies are listed under the products or services they offer.

You'll notice that some companies are listed more than once. That's because they offer more than one product or service. Also note that one company may give different addresses and phone numbers for separate divisions offering individual products and services. Where appropriate, trade names are listed in parentheses following a company's name.

Don't overlook your local phone directory; it's an excellent source for retail telephone equipment and service companies in your area.

If you know of companies, organizations, or other resources that should be included in future editions of *The Phone Book*, please send information to The Phone Book, c/o Tilden Press, 1737 DeSales Street NW, Washington, D.C. 20036

ADAPTERS/CONTROLLERS

Adapters and controllers provide two-line service for a single-line phone system, allowing such features as "hold" and "visual call indication," via an added light.

Mura Corp. ("MP-2L")
177 Cantiague Rock Road
Westbury, NY 11590
516-935-3640

Tone Commander Systems, Inc.
4320 150th Ave. N.E.
Redmond, WA 98052
206-883-3600

Viking Electronics, Inc.
406 2nd St.
Hudson, WI 54016
715-386-8861

AIRLINE TELEPHONE SERVICE

(See Chapter Seven.)

AirFone, Inc.
2030 M St. N.W.
Washington, DC 20036
202-659-0680

ANSWERING MACHINES

(See Chapter Four.)

Ansafone
Dictaphone Corp.
120 Old Post Road
Rye, NY 10580
914-967-7300

Answerex Inc.
10381 W. Jefferson Blvd.
Culver City, CA 90230
213-204-2493

Ford Industries ("Code-A-Phone")
16261 S.E. 130th St.
Clackamas, OR 97015
800-547-4683 (In AK, HI, OR: 503-655-8940)

Panasonic
Panasonic Way
Secaucus, NJ 07094
201-348-5200

Phone-Mate, Inc.
325 Maple Ave.
Torrance, CA 90503
213-320-9800

Radio Shack
(see local phone directory)

Sanyo Manufacturing Corp.
3333 Sanyo Road
Forrest City, AR 72335
501-633-5030

Sears Roebuck
(see local phone directory)

Sony Corp. of America
9 W. 57th St.
New York, NY 10019
212-371-5800

ANTIQUE TELEPHONES
(Originals and reproductions)

House of Telephones
15 E. Ave. D
San Angelo, TX 76903
915-655-4174

Paul Nelson Industries, Inc.
14 Inverness Drive East
Building 4
Englewood, CO 80112
303-779-5518

ANTIQUE TELEPHONES
(Cont.)

Pennsylvania Telephone Products
  Company, Inc.
328 Market St.
Lemoyne, PA 17043
717-763-1400

ANYTHING-TO-ANYTHING NETWORKS

(See Chapter Three.)

Western Union ("Easy Link")
One Lake St.
Upper Saddle River, NJ 07458
800-336-2510 (In VA, 800-572-2524)

Graphic Scanning Corp. ("Freedom
  Network")
329 Alfred Ave.
Teaneck, NJ 07666
800-336-3729 or 703-556-9397
  (In VA, 800-572-3358)

ITT ("FAXPAK")
FAXPAK Marketing, ITT
2 Broadway,
New York, NY 10004
800-424-1170 or 212-296-6520

ASSOCIATIONS

Association of Long Distance
  Telephone Companies
2000 L St. N.W.
Washington, DC 20036
202-463-0440
Represents long distance companies
that compete with AT&T. The
association can supply you with
names of long distance companies
that serve your area.

Electronics Industry Association
2001 I St. N.W.
Washington, DC 20006
202-457-4900
An association for manufacturers of
telephones and related equipment.

International Teleconferencing
  Association
P.O. Box 3706
Tysons Corner Branch
McLean, VA 22103
703-556-6115
Acts as a clearinghouse for tele-
conferencing users and suppliers.
Check with them before going it alone.

"I don't mind being put on
'hold,' but I think they've got
me on 'ignore.' "

—Troy Gordon

North American Telecommunications
  Association
511 Second St. N.E.
Washington, DC 20002
202-547-4450
NATA members build and sell
telecommunications equipment that
can be connected to the Bell System.
It used to be called the "North
American Telephone Association."

United States Independent Telephone
  Association
1801 K St., N.W.
Washington, DC 20006
202-872-1200
Represents most of the 1,500 independent phone companies in the U.S.

Videotex Industry Association
2000 L St. N.W.
Washington, DC 20036
202-544-5655
This newly formed association promotes and encourages videotex development. They maintain a small reference library.

AUTOMATIC DIALERS

(Note: Many multi-function phones contain an auto-dial feature.)

Buscom Systems Inc. ("Soft-Touch," "Port-A-Touch")
4700 Patrick Henry Drive
Santa Clara, CA 95050
800-538-8088 (In CA, 408-988-5200)

Dictograph Manufacturing Corp.
89 Glen Cameron Road
Thornhill, Ontario L3T1N8
Canada 416-881-0074

Hi-Tek Corp.
12311 Industry St.
Garden Grove, CA 92641
714-891-2566

Mitel Inc.
1745 Jefferson Davis Highway
Arlington, VA 22202
703-243-1600

Northern Telecom
640 Massman Drive
Nashville, TN 37210
615-883-9220

Teledial Devices, Inc.
125 Schmitt Blvd.
Farmingdale, NY 11735
516-293-8400

Telemate Communications Corp.
15 Park Row
New York, NY 10038
212-732-4888

Troller Corp.
445 N. Ravenswood Ave.
Chicago, IL 60640
312-271-1100

Zoom Telephonics Inc.
207 South St.
Boston, MA 02111
617-523-6280

A Matter of Degrees

Forecasts direct from the National Weather Service in Washington, D.C.:

For 10 selected Eastern cities:
202-899-3244

For 10 selected Western cities:
202-899-3249

BEEPERS

See "Paging Services."

BELL TELEPHONE COMPANIES

The local Bell telephone companies have been merged into seven regional holding companies, each responsible for a different section of the country.

Region 1 - Northeast:
New York Telephone
1095 Ave. of the Americas
New York, NY 10036
212-395-2121

BELL TELEPHONE COMPANIES

(Cont.)

New England Telephone & Telegraph
(serves Maine, Massachusetts, New
Hampshire, Rhode Island and Vermont)
185 Franklin St.
Boston, MA 02107
617-743-9800

Maine Office
1 Davis Farm Road
Portland, ME 04103
207-979-1247

Massachusetts Office
101 Huntington Ave.
Boston, MA 02199
617-743-9880

"Obscenity can be found in
every book except the
telephone directory."

—George Bernard Shaw

New Hampshire Office
1228 Elm St.
Manchester, NH 03101
603-645-2323

Rhode Island Office
234 Washington St.
Providence, RI 02901
401-525-2255

Vermont Office
One Burlington Square
Burlington, VT 05401
802-864-9977

Region 2 - Mid-Atlantic:
New Jersey Bell Telephone
540 Broad St.
Newark, NJ 07101
201-649-9900

Bell Telephone of Pennsylvania
One Parkway
Philadelphia, PA 19102
215-466-9900

Diamond State Telephone
3900 Washington St.
Wilmington, DE 19802
215-466-9900

Chesapeake & Potomac Telephone of
  Maryland
1 E. Pratt St.
Baltimore, MD 21202
301-539-9900

Chesapeake & Potomac Telephone of
  Virginia
703 E. Grace St.
Richmond, VA 23219
804-772-2000

Chesapeake & Potomac Telephone of
  District of Columbia
930 H St. N.W.
Washington, D.C. 20001
202-392-9900

Chesapeake & Potomac Telephone of
  West Virginia
1500 Mac Corkie S.E.
Charleston, WV 25314
304-343-9911

Region 3 - Southeast:
Southern Bell Telephone (serves
  Florida, Georgia, North Carolina
  and South Carolina)
Hurt Building
Atlanta, GA 30301
404-529-8611

Florida Office
666 N.W. 79th St.
Miami, FL 33152
305-263-2165

Georgia Office
125 Perimeter Center West
Atlanta, GA 30348
404-529-8611

North Carolina Office
Southern National Center
Charlotte, NC 28230
704-377-8772

South Carolina Office
1600 Hampton St. Building
Columbia, SC 29202
803-254-9011

South Central Bell Telephone (serves
Alabama, Kentucky, Louisiana,
Mississippi and Tennessee)
Headquarters Building
Birmingham, AL 35201
205-321-1000

Alabama Office
11 Metroplex Drive
Birmingham, AL 35202
205-321-1000

Kentucky Office
534 Armory Place Building
Louisville, KY 40232
502-560-1011

Louisiana Office
Canal Place One, 365 Canal St.
New Orleans, LA 70140
504-528-2000

Mississippi Office
First National Bank Building
Jackson, MS 39205
601-961-9011

Dial-It-Yourself

Some Bell telephone companies have set aside a special bank of numbers specifically for "Dial-It" services such as Dial-A-Joke, time, weather and sports information. The first three numbers are 976. Here are some numbers:

Time
976-1616
Weather
976-1212
Sports scores
976-1313
Jokes
976-3838
Santa Claus message
(a children's story off season)
976-3636
Chanukah message
976-2929
Lottery winning numbers
976-2020
Off Track Betting
976-2323
Stocks
976-4141
Sports features
976-2525

The call is local if you're in town or long distance if you're calling from out of town. Areas with telephone company dial-it services include New York City, Chicago, Detroit, Buffalo, New Jersey, Philadelphia, Connecticut, parts of California and Atlanta. For numbers used in each city, dial 976-1000 for a recorded announcement.

BELL TELEPHONE COMPANIES
(Cont.)

Tennessee Office
Green Hills Office Building
Nashville, TN 37215
615-780-9200

"An invention of the devil which abrogates some of the advantages of making a disagreeable person keep his distance."

—Ambrose Bierce

Region 4 - Midwest:
Ohio Bell Telephone
100 Erieview Plaza
Cleveland, OH 44114
216-822-9700

Michigan Bell Telephone
444 Michigan Ave.
Detroit, MI 48226
313-223-9900

Indiana Bell Telephone
240 N. Meridan St.
Indianapolis, IN 46204
317-265-2266

Illinois Bell Telephone
225 W. Randolph St.
Chicago, IL 60606
312-727-9411

Wisconsin Telephone
722 N. Broadway
Milwaukee, WI 53202
414-456-3000

Region 5 - Southwest:
Southwestern Bell Telephone (serves Arkansas, Kansas, Missouri, Oklahoma and parts of Texas)

Arkansas Office
1111 W. Capitol St.
Little Rock, AR 72201
501-371-9800

Kansas Office
220 E. 6th St.
Topeka, KS 66603
913-234-9911

Missouri Office
100 N. 12th Blvd.
St. Louis, MO 63101
314-247-9800

Kansas City Office
500 E. 8th St.
Kansas City, MO 64106
816-275-3000

Oklahoma Office
707 N. Robinson St.
Oklahoma City, OK 73102
405-236-6611

Dallas Office
308 S. Akard
Dallas, TX 75202
214-464-4647

Houston Office
3100 Main
Houston, TX 77002
713-237-7811

San Antonio Office
1010 N. St. Mary's St.
San Antonio, TX 78292
512-222-5861

Region 6 - Mountains and Great Plains:
Mountain States Telephone & Telegraph (serves Arizona, Idaho, Montana, New Mexico, Texas, Utah and Wyoming)
931 14th St.
Denver, CO 80202
303-624-2424

Arizona Office
3033 N. 3rd St.
Phoenix, AZ 85012
602-263-6411

Idaho Office
One Capital Center
Boise, ID 83702
208-343-7581

Montana Office
560 N. Park Ave.
Helena, MT 59601
406-449-3500

New Mexico Office
201 3rd St. N.W.
Albuquerque, NM 87102
505-765-6611

Texas Office
500 Texas Ave.
El Paso, TX 79901
915-543-4471

Utah Office
70 S. State St.
Salt Lake City, UT 84125
801-237-7200

Wyoming Office
2020 Capitol Ave.
Cheyenne, WY 82001
307-771-6141

Messages From Above

For the latest on stars, planets, volcanoes, and earthquakes, call Dial-A-Phenomenon from the Smithsonian Institution, Washington, D.C.:

202-357-2000

For astronomers, sky information from the Hayden Planetarium in New York City:

212-873-0404

Northwestern Bell Telephone (serves Iowa, Minnesota, Nebraska, North Dakota and South Dakota)
100 S. 19th St.
Omaha, NE 68102
402-422-2000

Iowa Office
909 High St.
Des Moines, IA 50309
515-286-5211

Minnesota Office
420 3rd Ave. South
Minneapolis, MN 55402
612-344-6565

Nebraska Office
100 S. 19th St.
Omaha, NE 68102
402-422-2000

North Dakota Office
105 5th St. North
Fargo, ND 58102
701-241-3150

BELL TELEPHONE COMPANIES

(Cont.)

South Dakota Office
125 South Dakota
Sioux Falls, SD 57102
605-336-2120

Pacific Northwest Bell Telephone
1600 Bell Plaza
Seattle, WA 98191
206-345-2211

Region 7 - Far West:
Pacific Telephone & Telegraph
140 New Montgomery St.
San Francisco, CA 94105
415-542-9000

Northern California Office
2150 Webster St.
Oakland, CA 94616
916-444-9000

Los Angeles Office
177 E. Colorado Blvd.
Pasadena, CA 91105
213-488-6500

Southern California Office
525 B St.
San Diego, CA 92101
714-232-4111

Bell Telephone of Nevada
645 E. Plumb Lane
Reno, NV 89502
702-789-6000

The following were associated with, but not controlled by, AT&T before divestiture:

Southern New England Telephone
227 Church St.
New Haven, CT 06506
203-771-5200

Cincinnati Bell, Inc.
225 E. 4th St.
Cincinnati, OH 45201
513-397-9900

BELLS

Loud ringing bells for the hearing impaired.

House of Telephones
15 E. Ave. D
San Angelo, TX 76903
915-655-4174

Northern Telecom
Advanced Telephone Products Div.
640 Massman Drive
Nashville, TN 37210
615-883-9220

Faraday, Inc.
805 S. Maumee
Tecumseh, MI 49286
517-423-2111

Touch Those Tones

The first Touch-Tone phone hit the commercial market in 1963. Now, more than 50 percent of all phones are Touch-Tone equipped. They are not only easier to use than rotary dials, they're also faster. An added benefit is that you can play songs on them. Try this ditty next December to get into the yuletide spirit:

6-6-6   6-6-6
6-#-7-8-6
9-9-9   99-5-5
5-5-5-7-4-5   6

BULLETIN BOARDS, COMPUTER

With a home computer, a telephone and a modem, it's possible to tap into hundreds of community bulletin boards (see Chapter Eight). New boards are going on-line all the time; unfortunately, though, others are disappearing. Local computer stores should have some numbers to get you started. For a free list of local bulletin boards, write:

Novation
18664 Oxnard Street
Tarzana, CA 91356
213-996-5060

If you want to keep up on new bulletin boards, a nationwide listing is available from:

The On-Line Computer Telephone
  Directory
P.O. Box 1005
Kansas City, MO 64111
($9.95 for four yearly issues)

To get started, try NASA's
  GASNET board:
301-344-9156

CALL-ACCOUNTING DEVICES

See "Toll-Call Monitors."

CALL DIVERTERS

If you're going to be somewhere else, have your calls follow. (Also, contact your local phone company for information about call forwarding service.)

Ford Industries, Inc.
P.O. Box 5656
Portland, OR 97228
503-655-8940

National Telephone & Electronics
7561 NW 77th Terrace
Miami, FL 33166
305-885-9423

CALL SCREENERS

Keep away those callers who don't know the secret code. See also "Multi-Function Telephones."

International Mobile Machines Corp.
  ("PriveCode")
100 N. 20th St.
Philadelphia, PA 19103
215-667-1300

Technicom International, Inc.
  ("Smartguard" multi-function
  telephone)
23 Old Kings Highway
Darien, CT 06820
203-655-1299

CATALOGS

If you don't have time to get to a phone store, fear not. You can order virtually everything you need—or want—from a catalog, the most interesting of which are listed here.

DAK Industries, Inc.
10845 Vanowen Street
North Hollywood, CA 91605
213-984-1559
800-423-2636
A good grab-bag of gadgets, including some high-tech phones and accessories.

CATALOGS

(Cont.)

Executive Mart
4 Tech Circle
Natick, MA 01760
617-655-4600

Heathkit
Benton Harbor, MI 49022
800-253-0570 (In AK, HI, MI, call
 616-982-3411)
This venerable kit-making company is
branching out into the telephone
business. For those who don't know
what a soldering iron looks like, some
phone accessories come already built.

Products That Think
One JS&A Plaza
Chicago, IL 60062
312-564-7000
800-323-6400
Perhaps one of the best catalogs for
futuristic phone equipment.

The Sharper Image
406 Jackson Street
San Francisco, CA 94111
800-344-5555
Sandwiched between the spy camera
and Samurai sword is one of the best
varieties of interesting phones and
accessories.

The Telephone Booth
One Tandy Center
Fort Worth, TX 76102
817-336-0616
Tandy, owner of Radio Shack, is getting into phones in a big way with a
chain of telephone stores. In the
meantime, its catalog, which is
heavier on designer models and accessories than high-tech items, offers
dozens of choices.

CELLULAR MOBILE RADIO

See "Bell Telephone Companies."
Also, check under "Radio Common Carrier" in local telephone
directory.

CHIMES

See also "Bells."

Telephonic Equipment Corp.
17401 Armstrong Ave.
Irvine, CA 92714
714-546-7903

Wheelock Signals Inc.
273 Branchport Ave.
Long Branch, NJ 00740
201-222-6880

"She had to have a telephone.
There was no one to whom she
wanted to talk, but she had to
have a telephone."

—Joan Didion in *Play It As It Lays*

CLOCK-RADIO TELEPHONES

Electronic Readout Systems Inc.
117 S. Franklin St.
Tampa, FL 33602
813-229-3200

Technidyne
8550 Katy Freeway
Suite 216
Houston, TX 77024
713-468-0200

Time Products International
Subsidiary of Herbert Kwok & Co.
8700 Waukegan Road
Morton Grove, IL 60053
312-470-8700

CLOCK TELEPHONES

Why not? You've heard of clock
radios.

Teleconcepts Inc. ("Gabbi-Clock")
22 Culbro Drive
West Hartford, CT 06610
203-525-3107

That's Showbiz

Dial-A-Song direct from Los Angeles
features new artists:

213-664-SONG

COMPUTERS, PERSONAL

Apple Computer Inc.
20525 Mariani Ave.
Cupertino, CA 95014
800-538-9696 (In CA, 800-662-9238)

Digital Equipment Corp.
129 Parker St.
Maynard, CA 01754
800-DIGITAL
Also makes a portable computer with
modem to connect with any phone line
while you're on the go.

IBM
Old Orchard Road
Armonk, NY 10504
800-631-5582 (In AK, HI, call
   800-526-2484)

NEC Home Electronics, Inc.
1401 Estes Ave.
Elk Grove Village, IL 60007
312-228-5900

Osborne Computer Corp.
36538 Danti Court
Hayward, CA 94545
415-887-8080

Radio Shack
Tandy Corp.
1300 One Tandy Center
Fort Worth, TX 76102
817-390-3700

Tymshare ("Scanset")
20705 Valley Green Drive
Cupertino, CA 95014
800-228-2028
Scanset isn't a full-blown computer,
but it will allow you to access data
bases over phone lines. It's ideal for
those who don't need the capacity of
(or want to spend the extra money for)
a computer.

CONGRESS

Here are committees interested in
telephone issues.

House of Representatives

Telecommunications Subcommittee
Room B331
Rayburn House Office Building
Washington, DC 20515
202-225-9304

Senate

Communications Subcommittee
130 Russell Senate Office Building
Washington, DC 20510
202-224-8144

CONSUMER GROUPS

Most of these groups can offer guidance on telephone-related issues, including problems relating to telephone companies.

Congress Watch
204 Pennsylvania Ave. SW
Washington, DC 20003
202-546-4996

Consumers Union (Washington office)
1511 K St. NW
Washington, DC 20005
202-783-6130

Your Tax Dollars at Work

Find out the status of congressional legislation by calling these recorded announcements:

Senate:
202-224-8541
(Democrats)

202-224-8601
(Republicans)

House of Representatives:
202-225-7400
(Democrats)

202-225-7430
(Republicans)

Telecommunications Consumer Coalition
105 Madison Ave.
New York, NY 10016
212-683-5656

Telephone Project
Box 12038
Washington, DC 20005
202-462-2520

CORDLESS TELEPHONES

(See Chapter Four.)

Cobra Communications
A Division of Dynascan Corp.
6460 W. Cortland
Chicago, IL 60635
312-889-8870

Electra Co.
300 W. County Line Road South
Cumberland, IN 46229
317-894-1440

Fracom/Rovafone International
2130 W. Clybourn St.
Milwaukee, WI 53233
414-933-6904

Kraco Enterprises Inc.
505 E. Euclid Ave.
Compton, CA 90224
800-421-1910 (in CA, 213-639-0666)

Midland International Corp.
1690 N. Topping
Kansas City, MO 64120
816-241-8500

Mura Corp. ("Muraphone")
177 Cantiague Rock Road
Westbury, NY 11590
516-935-3640

Newcomm Electronics ("Ultima")
1805 Macon St.
North Kansas City, MO 64116
816-842-7205

Pathcom Inc. ("Pacer")
24105 S. Frampton Ave.
Harbor City, CA 90710
213-325-7310

Radio Shack
(see local phone directory)

Uniden Corp. of America ("Extend-A-Phone")
15161 Triton Lane
Huntington Beach, CA 92649
714-895-1135

Webcor Electronics
28 S. Terminal Drive
Plainview, NY 11803
516-349-0600

CORDS

Available in stores that sell phones and accessories.

DATA BASES

(See Chapter Eight.)

BRS
Biographical Retrieval Services
1200 Route 7
Latham, New York 12110
518-783-1161
800-833-4704
A major data base vendor for business and educational use, BRS offers access to millions of abstracts on more than 65 data bases. Electronic mail is available, as is overnight delivery of printed searches. In addition, BRS/After Dark, which requires a one-time $50 subscription fee, is available for the home computer user. On-line costs for the After Dark service are as little as $6 per hour.

CompuServe
5000 Arlington Centre Boulevard
Columbus, Ohio 43220
800-848-8990
One of the most popular services for home computer and small business users, CompuServe (a subsidiary of the H&R Block tax people) offers a number of different newspapers, the Associated Press wires, business, financial and educational data bases, and electronic mail.

"I should never have invented the telephone if I had been an electrician. What electrician would have hit upon so mad an idea?"

—Alexander Graham Bell

Dialog Information Services, Inc.
3460 Hillview Avenue
Palo Alto, California 94394
800-227-1927
800-982-5838 (California)
The granddaddy of on-line information services, Dialog offers more data bases on more subjects—everything from patent abstracts to pollution abstracts—than any other firm. Owned by Lockheed, Dialog provides off-line printing and mail service, and covers more than 150 data bases housing more than 50 million abstracts.

Dow Jones & Company
P.O. Box 300
Princeton, New Jersey 08540
609-452-2000
If stocks and bonds, or the financial community in general, is your main interest, you already know all about Dow Jones. Instead of calling your broker for a quote, or waiting for the morning paper to read about grain futures, Dow Jones will give it all to you on the spot.

DATA BASES

(Cont.)

The Information Bank
1719 A Route 100
Parsippany, New Jersey 07054
201-539-5850
Here's all the news that's fit to
telecommunicate. This data base contains abstracts from the *New York
Times* and more than 70 other
newspapers and magazines.

"When at first this little instru-
ment appeared, consisting, as
it does, of parts capable of being put together by an amateur,
the disappointment arising
from its humble appearance
was only partially relieved on
finding that it was really able to
talk."

—James Clerk Maxwell
in "The Telephone," 1878

Mead Data Central
Mead Corp.
9333 Springboro Pike
Dayton, OH 45401
513-859-1611
Mead Data Central publishes Lexis,
the on-line legal resource, and Nexis,
a full-text search service that offers
access to a variety of newspapers,
magazines, and wire services. Both
use dedicated phone lines installed by
the company. Subscribers must use
special terminals and printers.

NewsNet
945 Haverford Road
Bryn Mawr, Pennsylvania 19010
215-527-8030
800-345-1301
At last count, NewsNet offered on-
line access to nearly two dozen
newsletters. The service, which has no
initiation charge and a $15 minimum
monthly fee, allows the scanning of
headlines, keyword searches in current or back issues, scanning indexes,
and reading sample issues. Among
the newsletters you'll find on
NewsNet are Fiber/Laser News, Coal
Outlook Marketline, and Television
Digest.

The Source
Source Telecomputing Corporation
1616 Anderson Road
McLean, Virginia 22102
703-734-7500
800-336-3366
The Source, owned by The Reader's
Digest, is one of the more popular services for home use. Included is a long
list of data bases, offering everything
from games and hobbies, travel and
entertainment, UPI news, professional investment services and electronic mail. Registration fee is $100
and there is a $10 monthly minimum
charge.

DECORATOR PHONES

(See Chapter Four.)

American Telecommunications Corp.
  ("Genie Phone")
9620 Flair Drive
El Monte, CA 91731
213-579-1710

Krone Inc.
9600 E. Arapahoe Road
Suite 270
Englewood, CO 80112
303-773-2619

Lippincott Industries Inc.
Building S/3
Spokane Industrial Park
Spokane, WA 99216
509-326-9111

Major Telephone Corp. of America
P.O. Box 1088
Reno, NV 89504
702-322-4266

Microcommunications Corp.
Subsidiary of Microsemiconductor
  Corp.
3307 Castor St.
Santa Ana, CA 92704
714-540-3700
Elegant models, many woodgrained.

Nichco Inc.
8660 Troy Township Road #4—R.R. 9
Mansfield, OH 44904
419-884-0123

Onyx Telecommunications Ltd.
505 8th Ave.
New York, NY 10018
212-239-4450
Classic French-style phones.

Paul Nelson Industries
14 Inverness Drive East
Building 4
Englewood, CO 80112
Everything from gumball phones to
oak antique wall phones.

Pierre Cardin Electronique
1115 Broadway
New York, NY 10010
212-255-7688
Even the great clothing designer gets
in on the action.

"The greatest nuisance among
the conveniences, the greatest
convenience among nui-
sances."

—Robert Lynd

Specialty Phones Inc. ("Phona-
  Duck," "Phona-Bass," etc.)
742 Cedar Way
Oakmont, PA 15139
412-828-7770

SPS Industries Inc. ("Modulo-Phone")
875 N. Michigan Ave.
Chicago, IL 60611
312-440-0275
Slim, trim, lightweight pastel-colored
phones.

Teleconcepts Inc.
22 Clubro Drive
West Hartford, CT 06110
203-525-3107
High-tech designs, including the
"Cleartalk" visible phone.

DECORATOR PHONES

(Cont.)

Teletronics United Inc.
2910 Rubidoux Blvd.
Riverside, CA 92509
714-682-1751

Unical Enterprises Inc. ("Futura"
   series)
9031 Slauson Ave.
Pico Rivera, CA 90660
213-949-9685

DIALERS

See "Automatic Dialers."

DIRECTORIES

Celebrity Publishing Inc.
P.O. Box 98
Suffern, NY 10901
Publishers of "The Travel and Vaca-
tions Toll-Free Directory," "The Na-
tional Toll-Free Directory," and "The
Shop at Home Toll-Free Directory."

"Toll-Free Digest"
Warner Books, $2.50
bulk orders: P.O. Box 690
New York, NY 10019

"National Directory of Addresses and
   Telephone Numbers"
240 Fenci Lane
Hillside, IL 60162
$24.95 + $2 shipping

DISCOUNT PHONE COMPANIES

See "Long Distance Discount
Telephone Companies."

EMERGENCY TELEPHONE DIALER

Mura Corp. ("Sage-1")
177 Cantiague Rock Road
Westbury, NY 11590
516-935-3640
When this small, lightweight unit is
hung from your neck like a necklace,
help via your phone is only a button
away.

"There is something about saying 'OK' and hanging up the
receiver with a bang that kids
a man into feeling that he has
just pulled off a big deal, even
if he has only called up central
to find out the correct time."

—Robert Benchley

FACSIMILE MACHINES

(See Chapter Three.)

Exxon Office Systems ("Qwip")
P.O. Box 10184
Stamford, CT 06904
800-327-6666 (In CT, 800-942-2525)

NEC America Inc.
532 Broad Hollow Road,
Melville, NY 11747
800-645-9836 (In NY, 516-752-9700)

Panafax Corp.
185 Froehlich Farm Blvd.
Woodbury, NY 11797
800-645-7486 (In NY, 212-364-1400)

THE YELLOW PAGES   •   FEDERAL

Pitney Bowes
9235 Pacific St.
Stamford, CT 06926
800-621-5199 (In IL, 800-972-5855)

Telautograph ("Omnifax")
8700 Bellanca Ave.
Los Angeles, CA 90045
213-641-3690

3M
3M Center
St. Paul, MN 55114
612-733-1110

Xerox
Stamford, CT 06904
203-329-8700

FACSIMILE SERVICES

(See Chapter Three.)

AT&T Overseas Facsimile
AT&T Long Lines
201 Littleton Road
Morris Plains, NJ 07950
201-631-1000

Western Union International Facsimile Bureau Service
One WUI Plaza
New York, NY 10004
800-221-7902 (In NY, 212-363-7762)

FEDERAL COMMUNICATIONS
COMMISSION

DOCUMENTS
The Downtown Copy Center, which operates under government contract, researches and copies FCC public documents for a fee.

Downtown Copy Center
1114 21 St. N.W.,
Washington, D.C. 20037
202-452-1422
Research: $10 per hour
Copying: 9 cents per page
Also has FCC telephone directory:
$1.54 per copy for postal delivery
$1.05 per copy if picked up

Freebies

Many companies have set up toll-free "800" numbers for the convenience of callers. The biggest users are airlines and hotels. However, most states have established numbers exclusively aimed at citizens within their states for information about food stamps, consumer protection, libraries, poison centers, child abuse and taxes. The federal government also has some "800" numbers that anyone in any state can dial. Call 800-555-1212 for more information on "800" numbers.

FCC Public Document Room
1919 M St. N.W.
Washington, DC 20554
Room 239
It has copy machines if you want to try your hand at ferreting out your own information.

HELP!
FCC Office of Consumer Assistance and Small Business can help you directly or tell you who can. Try the main numbers first.

Main Numbers:
202-632-7000 and 632-7260

FEDERAL COMMUNICATIONS
COMMISSION (Cont.)

If your telephone service is cut off:
202-632-7553

For queries about customer-owned equipment:
202-634-1833

We Predict You Will
Dial Your Horoscope

From the Big Apple, here's Dial-a-Horoscope. All numbers are in area code 212.

Aquarius
976-6161
Aries
976-5050
Cancer
976-5353
Capricorn
976-6060
Gemini
976-5252
Leo
976-5454
Libra
976-5757
Pisces
976-6262
Sagitarrius
976-5959
Scorpio
976-5858
Taurus
976-5151
Virgo
976-5656

Direct-distance dialing:
202-632-5550

Eavesdropping problems:
202-632-6990

The following are not attached to the consumer office but staff will answer your questions:

Marine services:
202-632-7175
For licenses: 717-337-1212

Mobile phones:
202-254-7055

Paging:
202-632-6400

Telex:
202-632-7265

Wireless microphones:
Non-licensed: 202-653-8247
Licensed: 202-632-7505

If FCC staffers can't help, you can go right to the top: call the FCC chairman, 202-632-6600

FCC REGIONAL OFFICES
Atlanta Region
101 Marietta Tower, Room 2111
Atlanta, GA 30303
404-221-6500
Mailing Address:
P.O. Box 1775
Atlanta, GA 30301

Boston Region
1500 Customhouse
165 State Street
Boston, MA 02109
617-223-7226

Chicago Region
Park Ridge Office Center, Room 306
1550 Northwest Highway
Park Ridge, IL 60068
312-253-0368

Kansas City Region
Brywood Office Tower, Room 320
8800 East 63rd Street
Kansas City, MO 64133
816-926-5179

San Francisco Region
211 Main Street, Room 537
San Francisco, CA 94105
415-974-0702

Seattle Region
3244 Federal Building
915 Second Avenue
Seattle, WA 98174
206-442-5544

"Well, if I called the wrong number, why did you answer?"

—James Thurber

FCC DISTRICT OFFICES

Anchorage District
1011 E. Tudor Road, Room 240
P.O. Box 2955
Anchorage, AK 99510
907-276-7455
907-276-5255 (Recorded Information)

Atlanta District
Room 440, Massell Building
1365 Peachtree Street, NE
Atlanta, GA 30309
404-881-3084/5
404-881-7381 (Recorded Information)

Baltimore District
1017 Federal Building
31 Hopkins Plaza
Baltimore, MD 21201
301-962-2728/9
301-962-2727 (Recorded Information)

Boston District
1600 Customhouse
165 State Street
Boston, MA 02109
617-223-6609 ((Public service)
617-223-0689 (Enforcement)
617-223-6607/8 (Recorded Information)

Buffalo District
1307 Federal Building
111 West Huron Street
Buffalo, NY 14202
716-846-4511/2
716-856-5950 (Recorded Information)

Chicago District
230 S. Dearborn Street, Room 3940
Chicago, IL 60604
312-353-0195/6
312-353-0197 (Recorded Information)

Cincinnati District
8620 Winton Road
Cincinnati, OH 45231
513-521-1790
513-521-1716 (Recorded Information)

Dallas District
Earle Cabell Federal Building
U.S. Courthouse, Room 13E7
1100 Commerce Street
Dallas, TX 75242
214-767-0761
214-767-0764 (Recorded Information)

Denver District
12477 West Cear Drive
Denver, CO 80228
303-234-6977/8
303-234-6979 (Recorded Information)

FEDERAL COMMUNICATIONS
COMMISSION (Cont.)

Detroit District
231 W. LaFayette Street
Detroit, MI 48226
313-226-6078/9
313-226-6077 (Recorded Information)

Honolulu District
Price Kuhio Federal Building
300 Ala Moana Blvd., Room 7304
Honolulu, HI 96850
808-546-5640

When Seconds Count

Nearly every local phone company has a "time" recording, giving you the local time in minutes in seconds. But where do *they* call to synchronize their watches? The U.S. Naval Observatory Master Clock in Washington, D.C., that's where. This recording, based on the government's near-perfect atomic clock, will give you the exact time within milliseconds:

202-254-4950

Houston District
New Federal Office Building
515 Rusk Avenue, Room 5636
Houston, TX 77002
713-229-2748
713-229-2750 (Recorded Information)

Kansas City District
Brywood Office Tower, Room 320
8800 East 63rd Street
Kansas City, MO 64113
816-926-5111
816-356-4050 (Recorded Information)

Long Beach District
3711 Long Beach Blvd., Room 501
Long Beach, CA 90807
213-426-4451
213-426-7886 (Recorded Public service)
213-426-7955 (Recorded-Enforcement)

Miami District
51 S.W. First Ave., Room 919
Miami, FL 33130
305-350-5542
305-350-5541 (Recorded Information)

New Orleans District
1009 F. Edward Herbert Federal Building
600 South Street
New Orleans, LA 70130
504-589-2095/6
504-589-2094 (Recorded Information)

New York District
201 Varick Street
New York, NY 10014
212-620-3437/8
212-620-3435 (Recorded-Enforcement)
212-620-3436 (Recorded-Public service)

Norfolk District
Military Circle
870 N. Military Highway
Norfolk, VA 23502
804-441-6472
804-461-4000 (Recorded Information)

"Is this the party to whom I'm speaking?"

—Lily Tomlin
as "Ernestine the Phone Operator"

Philadelphia District
One Oxford Valley Office Building
2300 East Lincoln Highway, Suite 402
Langhorne, PA 19047
215-752-1324

Portland District
1782 Federal Office Building
1220 S.W. Third Avenue
Portland, OR 97204
503-221-4114
503-221-3097 (Recorded Information)

St. Paul District
691 Federal Bldg. & U.S. Courthouse
316 North Robert Street
St. Paul, MN 55101
612-725-7810
612-725-7819 (Recorded Information)

San Diego
7840 El Cajon Blvd., Room 405
La Mesa, CA 92041
714-293-5478
714-293-5460 (Recorded Information)

San Francisco District
423 Customhouse
555 Battery Street
San Francisco, CA 94111
415-556-7701/2
415-556-7700 (Recorded Information)

Someone invented the
    telephone,
And interrupted a nation's
    slumbers,
Ringing wrong, but similar,
    numbers.

—Ogden Nash

Information Please!

For local phone numbers:
411 or 555-1212.

For phone numbers anywhere in
the U.S. and Canada:
(area code) + 555-1212.

For toll-free "800" number
information:
800-555-1212

For information or operator
assistance for TTD:
800-855-1155.

For international telephone rates
from AT&T:
800-874-4000 (In FL, **342-0400**)

San Juan District
San Juan Field Office
747 Federal Building
Hato Rey, Puerto Rico 00918
809-753-4567
809-753-4008 (Recorded Information)

Seattle District
3256 Federal Building
915 Second Avenue
Seattle, WA 98174
206-442-7653/4
206-442-7610 (Recorded Information)

Tampa District
Ralph M. Barlow, EIC
Interstate Building, Room 601
1211 N. Westshore Blvd.
Tampa, FL 33607
813-228-2872
813-228-2605 (Recorded Information)

HEADSETS

ACS Communications Inc.
250 Technology Circle
Scotts Valley, CA 95066
800-538-0742 (In CA, 408-438-3883

Danavox Inc. ("Stetomike")
6400 Flying Cloud Drive
Eden Prairie, MN 55344
612-941-0690

Save a Lobster, Only 50 Cents

When "800" numbers just won't do, try "900" numbers. With a new service by AT&T called "National Dial-It," the caller pays a flat fee of 50 cents no matter where he is. The most popular number is 900-976-1313, National Dial-It Sports. It's worth the price just to hear the latest scores from what could be the fastest mouth in the world. The TV show "Saturday Night Live" once used "900" numbers for viewers to vote on whether "Larry the Lobster" should be boiled live on national television. For a list of working "900" numbers dial 900-555-1212. That call is free. (P.S. Larry lived.)

David Clark Company Inc.
372 Franklin St.
Worcester, MA 01604
617-756-6216

Deka Inc. ("Symmetry")
1745 Dell Ave.
Campbell, CA 95008
408-866-4208

GTE AES
1820 South
Salt Lake City, UT 84104
801-974-8249

Plantronics
345 Encinal St.
Santa Cruz, CA 95060
800-538-0748 (In CA, 800-662-3902)

HOLD BUTTON DEVICES

(for home phones)

Telemate Communications Corp.
15 Park Row
New York, NY 10038
212-732-4888

Tone Commander Systems Inc.
4320 150th N.E.
Redmond, WA 98052
206-883-3600

Walker Equipment Corp.
P.O. Box M
Highway 151 South
Ringold, GA 30736
404-935-2600

HOME INFORMATION

DIAL-UP NETWORKS

See also "Data Bases".

GTE Telenet Communications Corp.
8229 Boone Blvd.
Vienna, VA 22180
703-442-1000

Tymnet
20665 Valley Green Drive
Cupertino, CA 94014
408-446-7000

INDEPENDENT PHONE COMPANIES

(Top Five Only)

See also listing for U.S. Independent Telephone Association under "Associations."

Centel Corp.
O'Hare Plaza
5725 N. East River Road
Chicago, IL 60631
312-399-2500

Continental Telecom Corp.
245 Perimeter Center Parkway
Atlanta, GA 30346
404-391-8000

GTE Corp.
1 Stamford Forum
Stamford, CT 06904
203-965-2000

"I can now buy not only a Mickey Mouse and Pac-Man phone but also one endorsed by Oleg Cassini, Bill Blass, or Oscar de la Renta. What cost $55 last year has now been reduced to $20 and ads have appeared for phones for as little as $7. And all this for what I used to pay $45 *per year* to rent. Telephones will become the 'steak knives' of the 1980s."

—Mark S. Fowler
FCC Chairman

Mid-Continent Telephone Corp.
100 Executive Parkway
Hudson, OH 44236
216-650-7000

United Telecommunications Inc.
2330 Johnson Drive
Shawnee Mission, KS 66205
913-676-3000

INTERNATIONAL RECORD CARRIERS

They handle international Telex, TWX, etc. (See Chapter Three.) Many companies listed below have local offices in major cities.

Cable & Wireless, Ltd.
420 Lexington Ave.
New York, NY 10017
212-490-0610

FTC Communications Inc.
90 John St.
New York, NY 10038
212-669-9700

GTE Telenet Communications Corp.
8229 Boone Boulevard
Vienna, VA 22180
703-442-1000

ITT World Communications, Inc.
67 Broad St.
New York, NY 10004
212-797-3300

RCA Global Communications, Inc.
60 Broad St.
New York, NY 10004
212-248-2121

TRT Telecommunications Corp.
1747 Pennsylvania Ave.
Washington, DC 20006
202-862-4556

International Dialing

Country and City Codes (* means city code not required)

American Samoa * 684
Andorra 33: All points 078
Argentina 54: Buenos Aires 1, Cordoba 51, Rosario 41
Australia 61: Canberra 62, Melbourne 3, Sydney 2
Austria 42: Graz 316, Linz 732, Vienna 222
Bahrain * 973
Belgium 32: Antwerp 31, Brussels 2, Ghent 91, Liege 41
Belize 501: Belize City *
Bolivia 591: Cochabamba 42, La Paz 2, Santa Cruz 33
Brazil 55: Belo Horizonte 31, Brasilia 61, Sao Paulo 11
Chile 56: Concepcion 42, Santiago 2, Valparaiso 31
Colombia 57: Bogota *, Cali 3, Medellin 4
Costa Rica * 506
Cyprus 357: Limassol 51, Nicosia 21, Paphos 61
Denmark 45: Aarhus 6, Copenhaen 1 or 2, Odense 9
Ecuador 593: Ambato 2, Cuenca 4, Guayaquil 4, Quito 2
El Salvador * 503
Finland 358: Helsinki 0, Tampere 31, Turku-Abo 21
France 33: Bordeaux 56, Lille 20, Lyon 7, Marseille 91, Nice 93, Paris 1,
      Strasbourg 88, Toulouse 61
French Antilles * 596
German Dem. Rep. 37: Berlin 2, Dresden 51, Leipzig 41
Germany, Fed. Rep. of 49: Berlin 30, Bonn 228, Essen 201, Frankfurt 611,
      Hamburg 40, Munich 89
Greece 30: Athens 1, Rhodes 241
Guam * 671
Guatemala 502: Guatemala City 2
Guyana 592
Haiti 509: Port au Prince 1
Honduras * 504
Hong Kong 852: Hong Kong 5, Kowloon 3
Indonesia 62: Jakarta 21
Iran 98: Abadan 631, Teheran 21
Iraq 964: Baghdad 1
Ireland 353: Dublin 1
Israel 972: Haifa 4, Jerusalem 2, Tel Aviv 3
Italy 39: Florence 55, Naples 81, Rome 6, Venice 41
Ivory Coast * 225
Japan 81: Hiroshima 822, Kyoto 75, Tokyo 3
Kenya 254: Nairobi 2

International Dialing (Continued)

Country and City Codes (* means city code not required)

Korea, Rep. of 82: Seoul 2
Kuwait * 965
Liberia * 231
Liechtenstein 41: all points 75
Luxembourg * 352
Malaysia 60: Ipoh 5, Kuala Lumpur 3
Monaco 33: all points 93
Netherlands 31: Amsterdam 20, Rotterdam 10, The Hague 70
Netherlands Antilles 599: Aruba 8, Curacao 9
New Caledonia * 687
New Zealand 64: Auckland 9, Wellington 4
Nicaragua 505: Leon 31, Managua 2
Norway 47: Bergen 5, Oslo 2
Panama * 507
Papua New Guinea * 675
Paraguay 595
Peru 51: Arequipa 542, Lima 14, Trujillo 44
Philippines 63: Manila 2
Portugal 351: Lisbon 19, Oporto 29
Romania 40
San Marino 39: all points 541
Saudi Arabia 966: Jeddah 2, Mecca 22, Medina 41
Senegal * 221
Singapore * 65
South Africa 27: Cape Town 21, Johannesburg 11, Pretoria 12
Spain 34: Barcelona 3, Madrid 1, Seville 54, Valencia 6
Sri Lanka 94: Colombo 1
Surinam * 597
Sweden 46: Goteborg 31, Stockholm 8
Switzerland 41: Berne 31, Geneva 22, Lucerne 41, Zurich 1
Tahiti * 689
Thailand 66: Bangkok 2
Tunisia 216: Tunis 1
Turkey 90: Ankara 41, Istanbul 11
United Arab Emirates 971: Abu Dhabi 2, Ajman 6
United Kingdom 44: Belfast 232, Cardiff 222, Edinburgh 31, Glasgow 41,
    Liverpool 51, London 1
Vatican City 39: all points 6
Venezuela 58: Caracas 2, Maracaibo 61
Yugoslavia 38: Belgrade 11, Zagreb 41

INTERNATIONAL RECORD
CARRIERS (Cont.)

Western Union International, Inc.
One WUI Plaza
New York, NY 10004
212-363-6400

"Reach out and touch
someone."

—AT&T ad campaign, circa 1980

INTRASTATE DISCOUNT
PHONE COMPANIES

See "Long Distance Discount
Telephone Companies."

JACKS

Allen TelProducts Inc.
2211 S. Susan St.
Santa Ana, CA 92704
714-546-3522

Crest Industries Inc.
6922 N. Meridian
Puyallup, WA 98371
206-927-6922

Lynn Electronics Corp.
915 Pennsylvania Blvd.
Feasterville, PA 19047
215-677-6700

Plantronics Inc.
345 Encinal St.
Santa Cruz, CA 95060
408-426-5858

Suttle Apparatus Corp.
P.O. Box 28
Lawrenceville, IL 62439
618-943-2315

LOCKS, TELEPHONE

Data-Link Corp.
P.O. Box 1145
El Cajon, CA 92022
714-448-6716

Technidyne
8550 Katy Freeway
Houston, TX 77024
713-468-0200

Woodmar Co. ("Touch-Lock")
Blue Hills Route
Dewey, AZ 86327
602-632-7492

"Reach out and crush
someone."

—Slogan among Justice Department
antitrust lawyers, circa 1980

LONG DISTANCE DISCOUNT
TELEPHONE COMPANIES

(Service available in most cities
unless noted.) See also
"Associations."

Allnet Inc.
101 N. Wacker Drive
Chicago, IL 60606
312-443-1444
(Chicago and Washington, D.C.)

Altcom
2633 E. Lake Drive
Seattle, WA 98102
203-328-0567
(Seattle)

Alternative Communications Corp.
3000 Winston Road
Rochester, NY 14623
716-442-2904
(Rochester)

American Telephone & Telegraph Co.
(AT&T Long Lines)
Long Lines Department
Bedminster, NJ 07921
201-243-3000

Business Telephone Systems
713 W. Saint Johns
Austin, TX 78752
512-459-1100
(Texas, Louisiana, Kansas)

Call U.S.
2104 United American Plaza
Knoxville, TN 37929
615-525-2666
(Knoxville)

Dial America
Talbott Tower
Dayton, OH 45402
513-224-9764
(Dayton)

Interstate Communications
910 First Ave.
West Point, GA 31833
404-645-1013
(Georgia, Alabama, parts of Tennessee)

LDX Inc.
900 Walnut St.
St. Louis, MO 63102
314-621-1199
(St. Louis)

When The Spirit Moves

If you're in need of a little inspiration—say, 30 to 40 seconds' worth—here are a few of the many numbers you can call:

Baton Rouge
Dial-A-Devotional
504-926-2897

Detroit
Dial-A-Prophet
313-581-5140

Houston
Dial-A-Bible Message
713-464-1951

Long Island
Dial-A-Prayer
516-691-1168

Louisville
Dial-A-Bible Moment
502-452-1515

Miami
Dial-A-Verse
305-443-6600

New Orleans
Dial-A-Devotion
504-482-0792

Portland
Dial-A-Daily Bible Reading
503-283-3020

St. Louis
Dial-A-Saint
314-421-4775

San Francisco
Dial-A-Truth
415-655-3796

Seattle
Dial-A-Meditation
206-624-8985

LONG DISTANCE DISCOUNT
PHONE COMPANIES (Cont.)

MCI Communications Corp.
1133 19th St.
Washington, D.C. 20036
800-243-2140

Microtel Inc.
P.O. Box 22167
Tampa, FL 33622
305-422-9932
(Florida)

> "America's best buy for a nickel is a telephone call to the right man."
>
> —Ilka Chase, actress & author

Mid Atlantic Communications Corp.
  ("Valu-line")
790 Boston Mills Road,
Hudson, OH 44236
800-682-8282
(Ohio)

Penn Telecom Inc.
Gibsonia, PA 15044
412-443-9500
(Pittsburgh)

Satellite Business Systems ("SBS
  Skyline")
8283 Greensboro Drive
McLean, VA 22102
703-385-6906

Savenet
720 S.W. Washington St.
Portland, OR 97205
503-241-0090
(Oregon)

Southern Pacific Communications
  Company ("Sprint")
One Adrian Court
Burlingame, CA 94010
800-521-4949 (In MI, 313-645-6020)

Starnet Corp.
3949 Ruffin Road
San Diego, CA 92123
714-569-4022

TDX Systems Inc. ("Econo-Call")
1920 Aline Ave.
Vienna, VA 22180
703-790-5300
(Washington, DC area)

Telecommunications Services Co.
675 Brookfield Road
Brookfield, WI 53005
414-784-6752
(Milwaukee area)

Teltec
21000 N.E. 28th Ave.
Miami, FL 33180
305-932-3031
(Miami area)

U.S. Telephone Communications Inc.
  ("U.S. TEL")
106 S. Akard St.
Dallas, TX 75202
214-741-1957
(Southwest U.S.)

U.S. Transmission Systems Inc.
("Longer Distance," "ITT-USA")
333 Meadowland Parkway
Secaucus, NJ 07094
800-526-7270

Western Union ("MetroFone")
One Lake St.
Upper Saddle River, NJ 07458
800-325-6000

Wylon
235 N. Wolcott
Casper, WY 82502
307-266-3627
(Wyoming)

MARINE RADIOTELEPHONE

Manufacturers

R.L. Drake Co.
540 Richards Ave.
Miamisburg, OH 45352
513-866-2421

ICOM America Inc.
2112 116th Ave. N.E.
Bellevue, WA 98004
206-454-8155

Okeanos Inc.
8361 Vickers St.
San Diego, CA 92111
714-565-2194

Standard Communications
P.O. Box 92151
Los Angeles, CA 90009
213-532-5300

Services

Comsat Maritime Services
950 L'Enfant Plaza
Washington, DC 20024
800-424-9152

METEOR BURST

Telcom
8027 Leesburg Pike
Vienna, VA 22180
703-893-7700

MODEMS

Modems connect your computer or terminal to the phone lines, allowing you to communicate with other computers, get information from data bases, etc. (See Chapter Eight.)

Anderson Jacobson Inc.
25 Olympia Ave.
Woburn, MA 01801
617-935-4251

"Never answer a telephone that rings before breakfast. It is sure to be one of three types of persons that is calling: a strange man in Minnesota who has been up all night and is calling collect; a salesman who wants to come over and demonstrate a new, patented combination dictaphone and music box that also cleans rugs; or a woman out of one's past."

—James Thurber

Carterfone Communications Corp.
1111 W. Mockingbird Lane
Dallas, TX 75247
214-630-9700

Commodore Business Machines
487 Devon Park Drive
Wayne, PA 19087
215-687-4311

MODEMS

(Cont.)

Digital Equipment Corp.
146 Main St.
Maynard, MA 01754
617-897-5111

Hayes Microcomputer Products Inc.
5835 Peachtree Corners East
Norcross, GA 30092
404-449-8791

Listen Carefully

If you want to check out your hearing, call the Dial-A-Hearing Test. If you don't hear the four beeps, it may be time for that annual checkup.

516-822-4121

MFJ Enterprises Inc.
921 Louisville Rd.
Starkville, MS 39759
601-323-5869

Mura Corp.
177 Cantiague Rock Road
Westbury, NY 11590
516-935-3640

Novation Inc. ("Cat" series)
18664 Oxnard St.
Tarzana, CA 91356
213-996-5060

Prentice Corp.
266 Caspian Drive
Sunnyvale, CA 94086
408-734-9810

Racal-Vadic
222 Caspian Drive
Sunnyvale, CA 94086
408-744-0810

MULTI-FUNCTION TELEPHONES

These have many features including auto dialing, call waiting, call forwarding, toll restriction, toll-call monitoring, speakerphones, etc. (See Chapter Four.) Some models are usable as PBXs for small businesses.

American Bell Inc.
Consumer Products
5 Wood Hollow Road
Parsippany, NJ 07054
201-428-7700
Operates more than 460 telephone retail stores around the country.

Basic Telecommunications Corp.
("DataVoice")
4414 E. Harmony Road
Fort Collins, CO 80525
303-226-4688

Code-A-Phone
Box 5656
Portland, OR 97228
800-547-4683

Comdial Telephone Systems ("Maxcom" series)
1180 Seminole Trail
Charlottesville, VA 22906
800-446-7661 (In VA, 804-973-2288)

"America has a Cadillac phone system, but we pay Rolls Royce prices for it."

—William G. McGowan
Chairman, MCI

Crest Industries Inc.
6922 N. Meridan
Puyallap, WA 98371
206-927-6922

GTE Telecommunication Systems
    Inc.
19 Old Kings Highway
Darien, CT 06820
203-655-6055

More Touch-Tone Songs

4 4-8 8 6-8-6 1
All a-round the mul-ber-ry bush

4 4-4 8 6 0-4
the mon-key chased the wea-sel

4 4-4 8 8 6 6 1
the mon-key thought 'twas all in fun

5 1 6 0-4
POP! goes the wea-sel

4-4 2-4 # 8
Hap-py birth-day to you,

1-1 2-1 9 8
Hap-py birth-day to you,

4-4 #-4 3 * *
Hap-py birth-day dear Ger-ry

4-4 3-1 2 1
Hap-py birth-day to you

ITT Telecommunications Corp.
Telecom Business & Consumer Com-
    munications Division
133 Terminal Ave.
Clark, NJ 07066
201-381-2828

Iwatsu America Inc.
120 Commerce Road
Carlstadt, NJ 07072
201-935-8580

NEC Telephones Inc.
532 Broad Hollow Road
Melville, NY 11747
516-752-9700

Northern Telecom Inc. ("SL" series)
P.O. Box 10934
Chicago, IL 60610
800-621-6476 (In IL, 800-572-6721)

Oki Electronics of America Inc.
4031 N.E. 12th Terrace
Fort Lauderdale, FL 33334
305-563-6234

Rolm Corp.
4900 Old Ironsides Drive
Santa Clara, CA 95050
800-538-8154 (In AK, HI, and CA,
    408-496-0550

Solid State Systems Inc.
1990 Delk Industrial Blvd.
Marietta, GA 30067
404-952-2414

Technicom International Inc.
    ("Smartguard")
23 Old Kings Highway South
Darien, CT 06820
203-655-1299

TIE/Communications Inc.
5 Research Drive
Shelton, CT 06484
203-929-7373

Toshiba Telecom ("Strata" series)
2441 Michelle Drive
Tustin, CA 92680
714-730-5000

Walker Telecommunications Corp.
    ("Reliant 32")
59 Remington Blvd.
Ronkonkoma, NY 11779
516-981-5050

PAGING SERVICES

(See Chapter Three.)
For local firms, look in your local
phone directory under "radio common carriers," or contact:

Telocator Network of America
1800 M St. NW
Washington, DC 20036
202-659-6446

International

PageWorld Communications Inc.
228 East 45th St.
New York, NY 10017
800-223-1260 or 212-286-8901

National

MCI Airsignal
2000 M St.
Washington, DC 20036
202-429-9666

National Satellite Paging Inc.
(Joint venture of Mobile Communica-
tions Corp. of America and National
Public Radio)
Mobile Communications Corp. of
    America
1500 Capital Towers
Jackson, MS 39201
601-969-1200

PageAmerica Communications Inc.
228 East 45th St.
New York, NY 10017
800-223-1260 or 212-286-8901

Telemet America Inc. ("Pocket-
    Quote" pager)
401 Wythe St.
Alexandria, VA 22314
703-548-2042

PHONEPHREAKS

Technology Assistance Program
147 W. 42 St. Room 603
New York, NY 10036
This address is a mail drop for the
group that publishes a newsletter six
times a year.

" . . . Why can't that telephone
ring? Why can't it, why can't it?
Couldn't you ring? Ah, please,
couldn't you? You damned,
ugly, shiny thing. It would hurt
you to ring, wouldn't it? Oh, that
would hurt you damn you, I'll
pull your filthy roots out of the
wall, I'll smash your smug
black face in little bits. Damn
you to hell."

—Dorothy Parker

"A Telephone Call"

PORTABLE COMPUTERS

See also "Computers."

Digital Equipment Corp.
Terminals Product Group
2 Mt. Royal Ave.
Marlboro, MA 01752
800-DIGITAL

Panasonic Company
Hand-held Computers
One Panasonic Way
Secaucus, NJ 07094
201-348-7000

PRE-RECORDED ANSWERING
MACHINE TAPES

Phonies Inc.
P.O. Box 2110
Cherry Hill, NJ 08003
609-424-6787
Amaze your friends: Let Ronald Reagan, Dolly Parton, or Groucho Marx sound-alikes answer your call.

PRINTER, TELEPHONE

For a complete listing of your calls.

Advanced Communications Inc.
  ("MP-2000")
532 Wendell Drive
Sunnyvale, CA 94086
408-745-7755

Machine, Speak To Me

Votan, a Fremont, California, company, builds devices that recognize your voice and then respond. You may call for an over-the-phone demonstration:

415-490-7979

PSYCHOLOGICAL STRESS
EVALUATOR

CCS Communications Control
633 Third Ave.
New York, NY 10017
212-697-8140
Also carries a full range of wiretapping and phone surveillance equipment.

PUBLIC UTILITY COMMISSIONS

These are the folks who set your local rates and monitor the quality of your service. (See Chapter Five.)

Alabama Public Service Commission
P.O. Box 991
Montgomery, AL 36102
205-832-5174

Alaska Public Utilities Commission
1100 MacKay Building
338 Denali Street
Anchorage, AK 99501
907-276-6222

Arizona Corporation Commission
1200 W. Washington
Phoenix, AZ 85007
602-255-3135

Arkansas Public Service Commission
400 Union Station
Markham at Victory
Little Rock, AR 72201
501-371-1718

Public Utilities Commission, State of
  California
State Building
San Francisco, CA 94102
415-557-0647

Public Utilities Commission of the
  State of Colorado
500 State Services Building
1525 Sherman Street
Denver, CO 80203
303-839-3181

Public Utility Control Authority
State of Connecticut
State Office Building
Hartford, CT 06115
203-827-1553

PUBLIC UTILITY COMMISSIONS

(Cont.)

Delaware Public Service Commission
1560 S. DuPont Highway
Dover, DE 19901
302-736-4247

Public Service Commission of the
District of Columbia
451 Indiana Ave., NW
Washington, D.C. 20001
202-727-3065

Florida Public Service Commission
101 E. Gaines Street
Tallahassee, FL 32301
904-488-1234

Flights of Fancy

If you happen to be wondering whether Canadian geese have been passing through the Denver area, the local Audubon Society will be happy to fill you in. For news of recent sightings, try Dial-A-Bird:

614-221-9736

Georgia Public Service Commission
244 Washington St., S.W.
Atlanta, GA 30334
404-656-4562

Public Utilities Commission of the
State of Hawaii
1164 Bishop St.
Suite 911
Honolulu, HI 96813
808-548-3990

Idaho Public Utilities Commission
Statehouse
Boise, ID 83720
208-334-3143

Illinois Commerce Commission
527 East Capitol Avenue
Springfield, IL 62706
217-782-7295

Indiana Public Service Commission
901 State Office Building
Indianapolis, IN 46204
317-232-2715

Iowa State Commerce Commission
Lucas State Office Building
State Capitol
Des Moines, IA 50319
515-281-3428

Kansas State Corporation Commission
State Office Building
Topeka, KS 66612
913-296-3355

Kentucky Public Service Commission
730 Schenkel Lane
P.O. Box 615
Frankfort, KY 40602
502-564-3940

Louisiana Public Service Commission
One American Place
Suite 1630
Baton Rouge, LA 70825
504-342-4427

Maine Public Utilities Commission
State House
Station 18
Augusta, ME 04333
207-289-3831

"Look, I'm a real person; I'm in the phone book."

—Steve Martin, in "The Jerk"

Free Calls to Uncle Sam

Here are some of the toll-free numbers provided by the federal government:

Consumer Product Safety Commission:
800-638-2772
(In MD, **800-492-8363;** AK and HI, **800-638-8333**)

Defense Department Fraud and Waste Hotline:
800-424-9098 (In DC, **693-5080**)

Environmental Protection Agency Pesticide Hotline:
800-531-7790 (In TX, **800-292-7664**)

U.S. Government Fraud Prevention Task Force:
800-424-5454 (Except DC)

Federal Elections Commission:
800-424-9530 (Except DC)

National Cancer Institute (Dept. of Health and Human Services):
800-638-6694 (In MD, 800-492-6600)

National Health Information Clearinghouse:
800-336-4797 (Except AK, DC and HI)

Highway Safety Hotline:
800-424-9393 (Except DC)

The IRS has "800" numbers for each state;
call **800-555-1212** for numbers.

Federal Highway Administration
National Ride Sharing Information Center:
800-424-9184 (Except DC)

Maryland Public Service Commission
American Building
231 E. Baltimore Street
Baltimore, MD 21202
301-659-6000

Massachusetts Department of Public
Utilities
100 Cambridge Street
Boston, MA 02202
617-727-3531

PUBLIC UTILITY COMMISSIONS

(Cont.)

Michigan Public Service Commission
6545 Mercantile Way
P.O. Box 30221
Lansing, MI 48909
517-373-3244

Minnesota Public Service Commission
780 American Center Building
160 E. Kellog Blvd.
St. Paul, MN 55101
612-296-2243

" . . . electronic communications represents the single most important area impacting on human society—there's really nothing else, I think, that comes close . . . "

—Edward Cornish
President, World Future Society

Mississippi Public Service Commission
Walter Sillers State Office Building
P.O. Box 1174
Jackson, MS 39205
601-961-5400

Missouri Public Services Commission
P.O. Box 360
Jefferson City, MO
314-751-3234

Public Service Commission of the
State of Montana
1227 11th Avenue
Helena, MT 59601
406-449-3008

Nebraska Public Service Commission
301 Centennial Mall South
Lincoln, NE 68509
402-471-3101

Public Service Commission of Nevada
Kinkead Building
505 E. King Street
Carson City, NV 89701
702-885-4180

New Hampshire Public Utilities
Commission
8 Old Suncook Road
Building No. 1
Concord, NH 03301
603-271-2431

New Jersey Department of Energy,
Board of Public Utilities
1100 Raymond Boulevard
Newark, NJ 07102
201-648-3290

New Mexico State Corporation
Commission
P.O. Drawer 1269
PERA Building
Santa Fe, NM 87501
505-827-4524

New York Service Commission
Empire State Plaza
Albany, NY 12223
518-474-7080

North Carolina Utilities Commission
P.O. Box 991
Raleigh, NC 27602
919-733-4271

North Dakota Public Service
Commission
State Capitol
Bismarck, ND 58505
701-224-2400

State of Ohio, Public Utilities
   Commission
375 South High Street
Columbus, OH 43215
614-466-3292

Oklahoma Corporation Commission
Jim Thorpe Building
Oklahoma City, OK 73105
405-521-3908

Public Utility Commission of Oregon
300 Labor and Industries Building
Salem, OR 97310
503-378-5849

Pennsylvania Public Utility
   Commission
P.O. Box 3625
Harrisburg, PA 17108
717-783-1741

Rhode Island Public Utilities
   Commission
Division of Public Utilities and
   Carriers
100 Orange Street
Providence, RI 02903
401-277-2443

South Carolina Public Service
   Commission
P.O. Drawer 11649
Columbia, SC 29211
803-758-3621

South Dakota Public Utilities
   Commission
Capitol Building
Pierre, SD 57501
605-773-3201

Tennessee Public Service Commission
Cordell Hull Building
Nashville, TN 37219
615-741-3939

We'll Take Manhattan, The Bronx, and Staten Island, Too

Although out-of-town information numbers are free, you might want to get local phone directories for cities you call frequently. Your own phone company will order phone books for you, and have them sent by mail. All you have to do is call them, pay the postal tab (usually under $5 a book), and you'll have your directories in your dialing fingers within two weeks.

Public Utility Commission of Texas
7800 Shoal Creel Boulevard
Suite 400N
Austin, TX 78757
512-458-0100

Public Service Commission of Utah
State Office Building
Salt Lake City, UT 84114
801-533-3009

Vermont Department of Public
   Service
120 State Street
Montpelier, VT 05602
802-828-2319

Commonwealth of Virginia, State
   Corporation Commission
P.O. Box 1197
Richmond, VA 23209
804-786-8967

Washington Utilities and Transporta-
   tion Commission
Highways-Licenses Building
Olympia, WA 98504
206-753-6423

PUBLIC UTILITY COMMISSIONS

(Cont.)

Public Service Commission of West
   Virginia
Capitol Building
Charleston, WV 25305
304-348-2980

Public Service Commission of
   Wisconsin
4802 Sheboygan Avenue
P.O. Box 7854
Madison, WI 53707
608-266-1241

Public Service Commission of
   Wyoming
320 W. 25th Street
Cheyenne, WY 82002
307-777-7427

REFURBISHERS

All are FCC-certified to fix your
telephone. (See Chapter Five.)

ALABAMA

Communications Equipment & Con-
   tracting Co.
Box 628
Union Springs, AL 36089
205-738-2000

ALASKA

Alaska Tele-Services
Box 855
Wasilla, AK 99687
907-376-2354

Employment & Training Center
2330 Nichols Ave.
Anchorage, AK 99504
907-279-6617

ARIZONA

V.T.S. Industrial Co.
PO Drawer MM
Salome, AZ 85358
602-859-3595

CALIFORNIA

B & J Enterprises
439 W. 19th St.
Costa Mesa, CA 92627
714-540-2274

David Burns
12112 Peoria Street
Sun Valley, CA 91352
213-768-0653

Colin Chambers
1528 Myra Ave.
Los Angeles, CA 90027
213-662-9000

Hegge Services
4554 Caterpillar Road
Redding, CA 96001
916-243-8341

Los Angeles Telephone Co.
2335 Westwood Boulevard
Los Angeles, CA 90064
213-470-3344

Pac-West Telecomm
5757 Pacific Ave.
Stockton, CA 95207
209-952-1236

Phones & Phones & Such
1580 Sebastopol Road
Santa Rosa, CA 95401
707-523-3123

U.S. Telecommunications
15346 Bonanza Road
Victorville, CA 92392
714-245-0281

COLORADO
Western Antique Telephone Supply
1535 S. Broadway
Denver, CO 80210
303-778-1717

FLORIDA
Communications Equipment Co.
605 S. 14th Street
Leesburg, FL 32748
904-787-7320

Dakel Inc.
843 Miramar Street
Cape Coral, FL 33904
813-542-3658

Precision Communications Services
2609 DeLeon Street
Tampa, FL 33609
813-870-0362

Telephone Equipment Co.
Box 596
Leesburg, FL 32748
904-728-2730

Telephone Products Co.
Box 6015
Clearwater, FL 33518
813-441-1515

Utility Marketing & Development Co.
Box 16987
Tampa, FL 33687
813-971-8870

Wintel Services Corp.
Box 9200
Longwood, FL 32750
305-830-3265

Zentmeyer Company
5312 W. Crenshaw
Tampa, FL 33614
813-885-5649

GEORGIA
Georgia Tel-Electronics
Walnut Street at U.S. 441
Cornelia, GA 30531
404-778-9292

ILLINOIS
Telephone Repair & Supply
1768 W. Lunt Avenue
Chicago, IL 60626
312-764-3817

Connections Are Everything

Remember: Any device you connect to the phone lines—telephones, answering machines, modems, speed dialers, or anything else— must have an FCC certification label showing the Ringer Equivalence Number (REN) and other information. It's not only illegal to connect an uncertified device, but it may ruin your phone service. You could be forced to call the phone company to put things right again—at your expense. See Chapter Five for details.

Tele-Services Co.
6210 Oakton Street
Morton Grove, IL 60053
312-967-6600

KENTUCKY
Central Services
Box 186
Kevil, KY 42053
502-462-2146

MARYLAND (Washington, D.C. area)
Stanwood Electronics
9421 Georgia Avenue
Silver Spring, MD 20910
301-565-2727

REFURBISHERS

(Cont.)

MINNESOTA
Gorecki Electronics
640 8th Street NE
Milaca, MN 56353
612-983-3180

MISSOURI
United Telephone Co.
311 Ellis Boulevard
Jefferson City, MO 65101
314-634-1511

Sorry, Wrong Number

Having an unlisted phone number will cost you a little extra money in most areas, but if you're intent on keeping your name out of the telephone directory, you can save that extra cost with a little trickery. The phone company doesn't specify how you must list your name: some people list their complete name, some list a last name and first initial, etc. And some people use fake names, which saves them the cost of having an unlisted number. Moreover, it alerts them when a phone salesperson calls. ("Oh no, this isn't Mr. Mongoose, this is the chauffeur. Mr. Mongoose is skiing in Geneva.")

NEBRASKA
Lincoln Tel & Tel
Box 81309
Lincoln, NE 68501
402-477-0716

NEW YORK
Bohnsack Equipment Co.
Woods Road, NY 12526
518-537-6213

Consolidated Communications
1163 Yonkers Avenue
Yonkers, NY 10204
914-776-1008

Metropolitan Tele-Tronic Corp.
134 W. 18th Street
New York, NY 10011
212-594-4030

Rotelcom
106 Central Avenue
Cortland, NY 13045
607-756-7511

Telephone Extension Corp.
13 Glen Drive
Bardonia, NY 10954
914-623-5544

NORTH CAROLINA
Brown Telephone Repair Service
3824 Weona Avenue
Charlotte, NC 28209
704-523-0420

Carolina Tel & Tel
122 E. St. James Street
Tarboro, NC 27886
919-823-9030

Communications Repair
3203 N. Davidson
Charlotte, NC 28205
704-334-3131

OHIO
Nicho Inc.
8660 Troy Twp. RD #4, RR 9
Mansfield, OH 44904
419-884-0123

Phonotronics Inc.
15229 South State Avenue
Middlefield, OH 44062
216-632-0236

OREGON
Phones Plus
656 Charnelton
Eugene, OR 97401
503-687-0111

PENNSYLVANIA
Telephone Engineering Co.
786 Main Street
Simpson, PA 18407
717-282-5100

"Divestiture wasn't our idea."
—AT&T Chairman Charles Brown
at 1982 annual meeting

United Telephone-Eastern Group
1170 Harrisburg Pike
Carlisle, PA 17013
717-243-6312

TENNESSEE
Richley Enterprises
105 Deeward
Hendersonville, TN 37075
615-824-1014

TEXAS
Bayless Industries
Box 500
Maud, TX 75567
214-585-2555

House of Telephones
15 E. Avenue D
San Angelo, TX 76903
915-655-4174

Netcom
Route 2, Box 321
Texarkana, TX 75501
214-794-2471

UTAH
Talk Shop Inc.
4835 Highland Drive
Salt Lake City, UT 84117
801-272-2562

VIRGINIA
Stromberg-Carlson Corp.
Box 7266
Charlottesville, VA 22906
804-973-2200

WASHINGTON
Lippincott Industries
Bldg 5/3, Spokane Industrial Park
Spokane, WA 99216
509-922-1783

WEST VIRGINIA
Telephone Repair Service
Box 588
Princeton, WV 24740
304-425-2734

WISCONSIN
Phoneco
Rt 2, Box 358C
Galesville, WI 54630
608-582-4124

SILENCERS

Keep the bells from ringing.

Saxton Products Inc.
215 N. Route 303
Congers, NY 10920
914-268-8646

Zoom Telephonics Inc. ("The Silencer")
207 South St.
Boston, MA 02111
617-523-6281

SPEAKERPHONES

For hands-free conversations. The days of separate speakerphones are coming to an end, being replaced by telephones with speakerphones built in. However, these devices are unique.

Controlonics Corp. ("Litephone")
5 Lyberty Way
Westford, MA 01886
617-692-3000
An infrared speakerphone that can be placed anywhere in the same room as the telephone without connecting wires.

Plantronics Inc. ("Phonebeam")
345 Encinal St.
Santa Cruz, CA 95060
408-426-5858
Similar to Litephone

STATE PUBLIC UTILITY COMMISSIONS

See "Public Utility Commissions."

SURVEILLANCE AND WIRETAPPING DEVICES

See also "Psychological Stress Evaluator."

Dektor Counterintelligence and Security Inc.
5508 Port Royal Road
Springfield, VA 22151

H.L.B. Security Electronics Ltd.
211 East 43rd St.
New York, NY 10017
212-986-1367

Law Enforcement Associates
Main St.
Belleville, NJ 07109
201-751-0001

New Horizons ("Dyna-Mike" wireless microphone)
1 Penn. Plaza, Suite 100
New York, NY 10119
800-824-7888 (In CA, 800-852-7777)

Scientific Systems
Box 716
Amherst, NH 03031
Sells plans to build infinity transmitter, wireless mikes, and the like. Write for catalog.

USI Corp. (wireless microphone)
P.O. Box 2052
Melbourne, FL 32901
305-725-1000

TECHNOLOGY ASSISTANCE GROUP

See "PhonePhreaks."

TELEPHONES

See also specific equipment and accessories: "Automatic Dialers," "Cellular Mobile Telephones," "Cordless Telephones," "Multi-Function Telephones," "Marine Radiotelephones," etc.

Retail Stores
Check local phone directory for locations of the following:

Radio Shack
Sears

PhoneCenter Stores (American Bell)
Local Bell Service Centers

Graybar Electric Company, Inc.
600 S. Taylor Ave.
St. Louis, MO 63110
314-531-4700
Graybar considers itself a "one-source" supplier for residential and business telephones and accessories.

House of Telephones
15 E. Ave. D
San Angelo, TX 76903
915-655-4174
The "House" carries a large supply of telephones and telephone gadgets. They are also an FCC-approved refurbisher.

TELEPHONE BOOTH MURAL

See Chapter Four.

Conversation Pieces
Cotswold House
St. James Square
Cheltenham, Glos., England

TELEX

See "International Record Carriers".

TELEX CONVERTERS

Allows your computer to send messages via the Telex network. (See Chapter Three.)

Chat Communications ("Chat II")
2438 Wyandotte St.
Mountain View, CA 94043
415-962-9670 or 415-965-2524

"It is my heart-warm and world-embracing Christmas hope and aspiration that all of us—the high, the low, the rich, the poor, the admired, the despised, the loved, the hated, the civilized, the savage—may eventually be gathered together in a heaven of everlasting rest and peace and bliss—except the inventor of the telephone."

—Mark Twain, 1890

Datapoint Inc.
9725 Datapoint Drive
San Antonio, TX 78284
512-699-7000

Envax Corp.
1401 Walnut Hill Lane
Irving, TX 75062
214-659-3800

TOLL-CALL MONITORS AND TIMERS

See also "Multi-Function Telephones."

Control Key Corp.
57 Pickering Wharf
Salem, MA 01970
617-744-0030

NEC Telephones Inc.
532 Broad Hollow Road
Melville, NY 11747
516-752-9700

TOLL-CALL MONITORS
AND TIMERS (Cont.)

TIE Communications Inc.
5 Research Drive
Shelton, CT 06484
800-243-2364

TOLL-CALL RESTRICTORS

Many multi-function phones include toll restrictors, too.

Bitek International Inc.
3200 E. 29th St.
Long Beach, CA 90806
213-426-5927

And That's No Joke

During 1980, customers of New York Telephone's Dial-A-Joke made nearly 300 million calls to the recorded service. More than two-thirds were made during business hours. It got so bad (or good, depending upon whether you're the phone company or not) that federal government employees ran up more than $5,000 a month of taxpayers' money just for their daily laugh. The feds were forced to install special equipment to prevent calls to Dial-A-Joke and similar services.

James Somers Company Inc.
527 S. Main St.
Geneva, NY 14456
315-789-7938

Micro Communications Corp.
3307 Castor St.
Santa Ana, CA 92704
714-540-3700

Phonetele Inc.
16139 Wyandotte St.
Van Nuys, CA 91406
213-988-5470

TeleMate Communications Corp.
15 Park Row
New York, NY 10038
212-732-4888

U.S. GOVERNMENT

See "Congress," "Federal Communications Commission." See also "Free Calls to Uncle Sam" (box), "Public Utility Commissions."

VIDEO-TELECONFERENCING

(See Chapter Three.)

Hilton Communications Networks
9880 Wilshire Blvd.
Beverly Hills, CA 90210
213-278-4321

Satellite Inc.
1660 L St. N.W.
Washington, DC 20036
202-331-1960

AT&T Picturephone Meeting Service
Bedminster, NJ 07921
201-234-7879

Inter-Continental Hotels
Pam Am Building
New York, NY 10166
212-880-1487

Western Union Videoconferencing
One Lake St.
Upper Saddle River, NJ 07458
800-325-6000

WNET Telecon (WNET-TV)
356 West 58th St.
New York, NY 10019
212-560-2067

HI-NET Communications Inc. (Holiday Inns)
3796 Lamar Ave.
Memphis, TN 38195
901-369-7539

NEC America Inc.
Radio & Transmission Division
2741 Prosperity Ave.
Fairfax, VA 22031
703-560-2010

VOICE MAIL

(See Chapter Three.)

BBL Industries Inc.
2935 Northeast Parkway
Atlanta, GA 30360
404-449-7740

Bell Telephone Companies
See listings under "Bell Telephone Companies."

Centigram Corp.
1294 Hammerwood Drive
Sunnyvale, CA 94086
408-744-1290

Commterm Inc.
10 Third Ave.
Burlington, MA 01803
617-273-5974

Radiofone
460 Sylvan Ave.,
Englewood Cliffs, NJ 07632
800-526-0844

Rolm Corp.
4900 Old Ironsides Drive
Santa Clara, CA 95050
800-538-8154 (In AK, HI and CA, 408-0550, ext. 3025)

VMX Inc.
1241 Columbia Drive
Richardson, TX 75081
214-699-1461

Wang Laboratories Inc.
One Industrial Ave.
Lowell, MA 01851
800-225-9264

VOICE SCRAMBLERS

Controlonics Corp.
410 Great Road
Littleton, MA 01460
617-486-3571

Datotek Inc.
13470 Midway Road,
Dallas, TX
214-233-1030

Motorola Inc.
1301 East Algonquin Road
Schaumburg, IL 60196
312-397-1000

VOICE STORE & FORWARD

See "Voice Mail."

WIRETAPPING

See "Surveillance and Wiretapping."

Area Code/Time Zone Calculator

Area Code/State	Time Zone	Area Code/State	Time Zone
201—NJ	EST	516—NY	EST
202—DC	EST	517—MI	EST
203—CT	EST	518—NY	EST
205—AL	CST	601—MS	CST
206—WA	PST	602—AZ	MST
207—ME	EST	603—NH	EST
208—ID	MST	605—SD	CST
209—CA	PST	606—KY	EST
212—NY	EST	607—NY	EST
213—CA	PST	608—WI	CST
214—TX	CST	609—NJ	EST
215—PA	EST	612—MN	CST
216—OH	EST	614—OH	EST
217—IL	CST	615—TN	CST
218—MN	CST	616—MI	EST
219—IN	EST	617—MA	EST
301—MD	EST	618—IL	CST
302—DE	EST	701—ND	CST
303—CO	MST	702—NV	MST
304—WV	EST	703—VA	EST
305—FL	EST	704—NC	EST
307—WY	MST	707—CA	PST
308—NE	MST	712—IA	CST
309—IL	CST	713—TX	CST
312—IL	CST	714—CA	PST
313—MI	EST	715—WI	CST
314—MO	CST	716—NY	EST
315—NY	EST	801—UT	MST
316—KS	CST	802—VT	EST
317—IN	EST	803—SC	EST
318—LA	CST	804—VA	EST
319—IA	CST	805—CA	PST
401—RI	EST	806—TX	CST
402—NE	MST	808—HI	PST
404—GA	EST	812—IN	EST
406—MT	MST	813—FL	EST
408—CA	PST	814—PA	EST
413—MA	EST	815—IL	CST
414—WI	MST	816—MO	CST
415—CA	PST	817—TX	CST
417—MO	MST	901—TN	CST
501—AR	MST	904—FL	EST
502—KY	EST	906—MI	EST
503—OR	PST	907—AK	PST
504—LA	CST	912—GA	EST
505—NM	MST	913—KS	CST
507—MN	CST	914—NY	EST
509—WA	PST	915—TX	CST
512—TX	CST	916—CA	PST
513—OH	EST	918—OK	CST
515—ID	CST	919—NC	EST